CHARLENE SANDS

WORTH THE RISK

HARLEQUIN®
entertain, enrich, inspire™

Recycling programs
for this product may
not exist in your area.

ISBN-13: 978-0-373-73203-6

WORTH THE RISK

CHARLENE SANDS

is a _USA TODAY_ bestselling author of thirty-five romance novels, writing sexy contemporary romances and stories of the Old West. Her books have been honored with the National Readers's Choice Award, the CataRomance Reviewers' Choice Award and she's a double recipient of the Booksellers' Best Award. She belongs to the Orange County Chapter and the Los Angeles Chapter of RWA.

Charlene knows a little something about true romance—she married her high school sweetheart! When she's not writing, she enjoys sunny Pacific beaches, great coffee, reading books from her favorite authors, spoiling her two cats and loving up her new baby granddaughters! You can find her on Twitter and Facebook. Be sure to visit her website for fun blogs and her ongoing contests at www.charlenesands.com.

This book is dedicated to my dear pals at LARA.
Many thanks for your constant support,
friendship and encouragement.
I appreciate every member of the chapter!

These wonderful people include:
Debbie Decker, Tanya Hanson, Robin Bielman,
Kathy Bennett, Lynne Marshall, Ericka Scott,
Maria Seager, Erica Barton, Dee J. Adams,
Eden Bradley, Jennifer Haymore, Carol Ericson,
Linda O. Johnston, Samantha Le, Allison Morse,
Christine London, Sandy Robinson, Jody Brightman,
Roz Lee, Robena Grant and Christine Ashworth.
To Rick Ochocki for always making us laugh at the
meetings and to so many others! You all rock!

One

A woman's boots.

They sat on the floor, next to the bed. A fancy curlicue design stitched on smooth chocolate leather trailed to the top of the zippered knee-highs. Seeing them brought a smile to Jackson Worth's lips. He lifted his arms quietly, stretching out while trying not to awaken his sleeping companion. Images invaded his mind of how sexy she'd looked wearing those boots and how turned on he'd been sliding them off her coltish legs. Her short skirt and scoop-necked top had come next, with very little effort on his part, as he recalled.

It didn't make a lick of sense. But he couldn't deny that after taking one look at his sister-in-law's best friend, Sammie Gold, approaching him at the hotel bar last night, with her familiar sweet smile, slender hips swaying and those incredible boots catching the overhead lighting, he'd been thunderstruck with lust.

But Jackson Worth was no fool. There'd be hell to pay for

what he'd done. He'd hear it from both his brothers, Clay and Tagg, but the worst of the wrath would come from Callie. Tagg's wife would take his head off and probably threaten to disown him.

Bright sunshine seeped in through the drapes and he closed his eyes, trying to ward off the headache pounding in his skull. The woman beside him on the king-size bed stirred and the scent of jasmine filled the air. Jackson breathed it in, and damn if his sated body didn't react, just from the sweetness.

Never before had he mixed business with pleasure, but this time, he'd outdone himself.

Sammie rolled over and her arm flopped onto his chest, her fingers on his skin, soft and possessive. She murmured something in her sleep that sounded too much like "boot-scooting boogie."

He glanced at the top of her pixie-cut, brown hair with colors of caramel, chestnut and rum blending like those of a rare gem. She was cute but not the kind of woman he usually dated. He winced at how that sounded, even to him.

He hadn't dated her. He'd slept with her.

Yep, Callie wasn't going to be happy when she found out. Without giving Jackson so much as a verbal warning to be on his best behavior, his sister-in-law had asked a favor of him, giving him her full trust.

Sammie's had it rough lately. She's lost her father and her business. Take her under your wing, Jackson. Help her. Please. It means a lot to me.

He'd blown that trust to hell.

Slowly, Sammie lifted her head off the pillow. Disoriented, she peered at him with deep brown eyes. "Jackson?"

"Morning, darlin'."

Her gaze darted around the elegant room. She blinked and refocused, then shook her head to clear it. All the color drained from her face and her eyes grew round as poker chips. She lifted herself up, the covers falling away from her unclothed body. Her breasts appeared, small, round and firm. Jackson silently groaned. If she were any other woman, they'd be halfway to heaven again this morning.

With a gasp, she looked down and grabbed the sheets to her chest. "Oh, no!" She sent him a questioning stare, blinking rapidly. "We didn't."

It wasn't the usual reaction he received from a woman after a night of great sex. "Apparently, we did."

She made an unfeminine groan and searched the room, looking for some sign of familiarity. "Where am I?"

"Paris."

She gulped air and her voice squeaked. "France?"

This was worse than he thought. "Las Vegas."

She collapsed against the back of the bed, her head cushioned by a feather-down pillow that billowed when she landed. She looked up at the ceiling, clutched the covers to her chin and muttered, "How did this happen?"

He was pretty sure it was a rhetorical question, but Jackson had the need to answer her anyway. With his head propped in his hand and elbow braced on the bed, he met her tentative eyes. He gave her the only explanation that would make any sense.

"Boots."

Sammie's muddled brain began to clear and through the haze she remembered coming to Las Vegas for a shoe convention. Her best friend, Callie Worth, had insisted that, because Jackson was in Las Vegas at the same time, she meet with him. Jackson had a good head for business. Jackson could help get her out of the financial mess she was in. Jackson could give her sound advice. Sammie had been robbed by her last boyfriend, an accountant who'd known how to juggle numbers and her heart—before absconding with nearly everything she'd owned.

She'd felt like a gullible idiot to have believed his lies.

She still felt that way, only now she had Jackson Worth to contend with, too.

Ever since her father had died a few months ago, Sammie hadn't made good judgment calls. But this might have been the dumbest thing she'd ever done...sleeping with her best friend's brother-in-law.

She spotted her clothes on the floor. They painted a vivid trail of lust to the bed. Her blouse, her skirt, her bra and her thong panties were strung like drying clothes on the line, one right after the other. A whimper, bordering on panic, rose from her throat. "How much champagne did I drink last night?"

She cringed, waiting for his answer.

He seemed to be calculating in his head. "Not that much...maybe two glasses."

Her mouth dropped open. "I—I don't normally drink. It affects me. I get, uh—"

He sent her a knowing look. "Wild and sexy?"

"Oh, no, did I seduce you?"

A smile caught the corners of his mouth. "It was mutual, Sammie. You don't remember?"

He'd been helpful, that much she remembered. They'd spoken business for half the night at the bar and they'd had some laughs, too. Then the champagne had arrived. After the first glass, she'd been fine, but she should have stopped at one. Having two glasses of the good stuff, with her sensitivity to alcohol and her slight frame...well, she should have known better.

Sammie had traveled from Boston a few months ago to attend Callie's wedding and had met Jackson then. They'd had several conversations and had developed a cordial friendship. He was devastating to look at. Gorgeous with a capital *G*. He was so out of her league that she'd never entertained thoughts of being anything more than casual friends.

She glanced at the silk sheets, the expensive room and the man who was probably buck-ass naked under the covers beside her. Somewhere between the elevator ride up to the room and Jackson peeling off her boots, her mind went a little fuzzy.

Oh, boy. "Not really. I don't remember…much." She sighed. "I shouldn't have had that second glass of champagne."

Jackson stroked her arm, his finger making circles just above her elbow. She trembled from his touch. A jolt of throbbing heat pulsed between her thighs and her memory cleared for a second. She remembered *something*…how her body reacted when he touched her. "It's a little late for that confession."

He was right. Last night at the bar she'd thrown caution to the wind. Tired of being Miss Goody Two-shoes, the bridesmaid and never the bride, and tired of denying that Jackson Worth was the sexiest man she'd ever laid eyes on, she'd done something totally out of character. She'd wrapped herself around Jackson on the dance floor and kissed him. He must have thought her needy and pathetic. "Th-that's me, always late to the party."

"Sammie," he said, his rasp deep and low enough to remind her how much she was missing out on by not remembering last night, "just so we're straight—you *wanted* to be at the party."

"I, uh…I know." What woman in her right mind wouldn't want to be?

She squeezed her eyes shut. She should have been more cautious. She blamed her behavior on losing her father and her business in a short span of time. But getting real with herself meant facing the truth. Last night she'd needed an ego boost and broad-shouldered, blue-eyed, sandy-haired hunk Jackson Worth was just the man to lift her out of the dumps. Not only was he an eyeful, but he'd been sweet, helpful and attentive. The combination had been irresistible.

Sleeping with Jackson was a stupid move—but not remembering all of it? Now that was just plain wrong. She was experiencing the guilt without as much as a hot spicy memory to go along with it. Now, she'd never know. And there would be no repeats of last night.

Yesterday she'd gone to the annual shoe convention hoping to muster some interest in her failing business. The economy was slumping and only the stronger companies were surviving. No one was interested in infusing capital in her small, unique boutique.

No one…except Jackson Worth.

Then it dawned on her. Her head spun and her eyes widened with realization. "Oh, my goodness, Jackson. We're… *partners*."

Jackson's mouth quirked with a quizzical smile, then he sighed deeply. "We made a deal *before* the champagne arrived, darlin'. You signed on the dotted line. Boot Barrage is now half mine."

Sammie lay in bed, her head cushioned on the pillow, listening to the crank of the faucet being turned on in the next room. The rush of water filled her ears and as the shower door opened then closed with a definite click, she didn't have to imagine what Jackson Worth looked like in the buff. No, five minutes ago he'd bounded off the bed in his birthday suit, beautifully tan, with the greatest backside she'd ever seen on a guy, and sauntered toward the bathroom.

"You sure you don't want to go first?" he'd asked.

She'd crawled farther under the sheets, shaking her head.

"No, you go first. I'd rather wait." Now she lay on the bed, her pulse pounding in her ears. For a girl who'd wanted to make a fresh start on a new life, she'd really put her foot in it. Among other things.

Sweet heaven.

A tremble erupted throughout her body like small aftershocks hitting one right after the other as the heavy weight of her indiscretion slowly sank into her brain. She tried taking deep breaths to calm her wayward nerves. It didn't work. Her breaths came out in short rapid bursts.

Then she remembered her yoga instruction, something she'd come to rely on when Allen the Loser had accounted his way out of her life, taking with him the bulk of her hard-earned cash. Slowly she sat up on the bed and swiveled to plant her feet on the floor. She stood, circled her arms above her head, stretching out until her fingertips touched, pinkies down, and inhaled slowly, deeply, letting oxygen fill her lungs. Then just as slowly, with finesse she'd learned from the yoga master, she let her breath out smoothly as she lowered her arms and hinged her body in half until her fingers touched her toes. Better. Much better. She repeated the movements several times. Tension rolled off her. Her fuzzy head cleared and the rapid beats of her heart ebbed to a restful rate.

It was amazing how well the technique worked on her.

For the short term anyway.

She was certain she'd have many more moments of anxiety. Her life was about to change forever. Moving across the country and starting up a new venture in an unfamiliar town was enough to make her anxious. And spending the night with Jackson, her new partner, and having to face him on a regular basis wasn't exactly the best-case scenario for a girl who'd blundered with her last love affair.

So far she was batting a big fat zero in her new life.

The peaceful hum of water ceased with another turn of the faucet, and the shower door clicked open. Sammie sank back onto the bed, lifting the sheets to her chin, making sure her naked self was adequately covered. Instead of picking up her clothes and getting dressed, she'd been focused on yoga. Ironically, all of the peace she'd gained in the past few minutes was effectively wiped away as the door to the bathroom opened and Jackson strode out.

He wore a plush robe the color of rich dark ink. Black suited him, and the day-old stubble on a chiseled face and wet, blond-streaked hair curling at his collar put him on par with a *GQ* model. But then, she'd already known that about Jackson Worth. He wore his clothes with style, he had a smile that could melt Arctic ice and, darn him, he had a charming personality that would set any female's mind spinning. The bottom line…Jackson was dreamy and dangerous and last night all of her internal warning signals had malfunctioned.

He carried a snowy robe in hand and tossed it onto the bed. It landed beside her in a heap of marshmallow softness. "Maybe you should get dressed," he said, his usual air of confidence a little shaken. "We need to talk."

Without waiting for her response, he moved to the window to allow the daylight in and caught a glimpse of a replica of the Eiffel Tower. With Jackson gazing out the window, she hurried her arms into the robe and tied it around her waist. Snatching her clothes off the floor, she headed toward the bathroom.

Her shower was quick and efficient. If circumstances were different, she would have luxuriated in the giant-sized marble enclosure with three directional faucets and lingered under the waterfall-like spray. She would have lathered herself with smooth-as-silk body wash and then treated her limbs to a citrus lotion massage. But Jackson was waiting and they had some serious talking to do.

She dressed in the clothes she'd worn to the convention yesterday, a little rumpled now from their night on the floor. With fingers gingerly moving through her hair, the thick, short layers fell back into place without much fuss. There was something to be said about good-hair days even when all else seemed to be going downhill.

She padded out of the bathroom in bare feet and noted Jackson was still standing by the window, but this time with a coffee cup in his hand. Sometime during her shower, room service had arrived. It always amazed her how magic seemed to happen to wealthy people and how much they took it for granted. With a snap of fingers, their every wish was granted.

Perhaps it was a good thing that Jackson was wealthy though, because he, unlike so many others that had refused her, had entered into a business arrangement with her. They were partners now, and Sammie had no illusions about his reasons. Normally, a cattle baron with investments in major real estate developments and the stock market wouldn't give a small-time boot seller the time of day, but Jackson was doing Callie a favor by backing Sammie's boutique. It made Sammie even more determined to make her business a success. She didn't want to disappoint Callie or have the Worth family look upon her as a charity case.

The dining table was set for two with white linens and a cheery vase of flowers. A vast assortment of breakfast foods covered the surface from end to end. Her appetite had waned the second she'd woken up next to Jackson, but now, after a good cleansing had given her a slightly better outlook on life, she heeded her stomach's grumble for nourishment. Those white-chocolate raspberry muffins were calling to her.

Jackson turned from the window to meet her eyes. His

gaze slid up and down her body, then his lips came together in a smile he couldn't hide. He quickly took a sip of his coffee.

"What?" she asked.

He gave his head a quick shake. "You don't want to know."

"I do," she blurted.

His eyes raked over her one more time, then he shrugged, as if giving her the answer wouldn't be the end of the world. "You look cute."

"Cute?" She glanced down at the cream-and-brown plaid pleated skirt and narrow tailored ivory blouse she'd tucked into it. The whole ensemble was designed to be worn with a solid cream blazer and her classic brown zippered knee-high boots, which tied the entire outfit together. She'd dressed for the convention to show how an entire look can be created and changed simply by wearing the right boots. It all came down to the power of the boot.

She wiggled her bare toes. Her boots were on Jackson's side of the bed. Her blazer was slung across a wing chair in the far corner of the room. No boots, no power. What was left was *cute?*

"You hungry?" he asked, glancing away from her toward the dining area.

"Yes. I could eat."

He gestured for her to go first. She moved across the room and took a seat at one end of the table. Jackson, still in his plush robe, sat down adjacent to her. He poured her coffee and waited for her to sip it. Once. Twice. The French roast was pure heaven, warming her throat and giving her the fortification she needed to get through this conversation.

His eyes stayed on her with interest and a surge of uneasiness gripped her. "What's up?" she said.

Jackson smiled again, that killer I-know-something-you-don't-know smile. "You *really* don't want to know."

She swallowed coffee so fast it burned her throat. Her traitorous eyes dipped below his waist, not that she'd see anything beyond the table's edge, but the intent was there and Jackson noticed.

"Oh."

"Listen," he began, shifting in his seat to face her fully. "I'm not the kind of guy to kiss and tell, but especially now, because of my relationship with Callie—and *yours*—I think it's best if we put last night behind us. It was a mistake and I take full responsibility."

Sammie winced inwardly. She knew what he was getting at, but for a man to say sleeping with her was a mistake was hard to hear, regardless of the man. But to hear it coming from Jackson Worth was really a slam to her ego. "It's not entirely your fault, Jackson. I played a part in it. Not that I remember...too much."

Jackson pulled a deep breath into his lungs as his eyes gleamed with private knowledge. "That's probably a good thing."

Why? Was it that good between them? Or that bad? She didn't have the nerve to ask.

She bet few if any of his women had forgotten what it was like to make love with Jackson. And if his ego was bruised, he wasn't letting on. Sammie wished she'd had a memory to take with her of a night she'd often fantasized about, but that wasn't the most important thing now.

"I really want a fresh start in Arizona. Callie's friendship is important to me. We'll be seeing a lot of each other and I would rather not lie to her, but not telling isn't exactly the same as lying, is it?"

"No, it's not. It'll be our little secret. No one has to know what happened and we'll move on from here, Sammie."

"Okay, we'll keep it a secret. I'm not one to go bragging either. I mean, it was just sex, right?"

Jackson began to nod and then stopped himself. His lips pursed. "I'm taking the fifth. Any man in his right mind wouldn't answer that question."

Sammie smiled for the first time since she'd opened her eyes this morning. "You're a wise man."

"Am I?" His gaze swept over her again and Sammie felt the heat down to her bones.

"You think I'm *cute*."

He grinned. "Cute can be sexy."

"Obviously."

He laughed.

She grabbed a muffin and took a big bite. She was feeling a little better now that they'd cleared the air. Neither one of them had any expectations, which was half the battle. The other half was to remember that Jackson Worth was her business partner and strictly off-limits. She could do that. She had to—there was no other option.

After breakfast, Jackson came out of the bathroom dressed in dark slacks and a western shirt. He'd offered to drive her to the motor hotel to pack her belongings and then take her to the airport to catch her flight to Boston. He plopped his Stetson on his head, looking like a Worth through and through as he stood by the bed, arms folded, watching her slip on her brown leather boots.

"There," she said, closing up the long zipper and straightening to full height, adjusting her feet in the boots. She met his eyes as she put on her blazer and gave her hair a toss. "I'm ready to go."

He glanced at her boots and then lifted his gaze to follow the contour of her legs. He had the oddest expression on his face but quickly shook it off. He took her hand and led her out the door. "Let's get outta here."

They'd made a pact and the old cliché held true. What happens in Vegas…

Sharing a secret with Jackson Worth could be thrilling. If only it wasn't so darn necessary.

Two

It was early fall back in Boston, just when the leaves were starting to turn and the entire city was awash with burnt-orange and gold foliage. It was by far Sammie's favorite time of year, when cooler air replaced summer humidity and fresh breezes rustled the trees. But there was no rustling of trees in Arizona. Not today anyway. The air was still and the land desolate but for the vegetation and shrubbery that had been transplanted to the desert from more tropical climes.

She would miss her hometown, but her life was no longer there and as soon as she'd landed at Sky Harbor Airport yesterday and stepped foot on Arizona soil, new excitement, a thrill she hadn't felt for a long time, surged through her system. This was it—her chance to make a fresh start. Her life would be here now and she had every intention of looking toward the future.

She stood in the middle of the large empty storefront, her eyes darting from the shiny hardwood flooring covering the expanse of the room, to the clean, unadorned walls. She took in the subtle scent of fresh paint. Lifting her head, she viewed thick beams of wood crisscrossing the ceiling, giving it a rustic charm. The place was perfect and in that perfection, she also saw Jackson Worth's handiwork. He'd picked a great Scottsdale location for the boutique, right smack in the heart of prime shopping for the middle to upper class of Phoenix society.

The sound of her boots clicking against the floors echoed her movements as she walked toward the front door. It was a lonely sound, one that reminded her of all she'd lost, of the emptiness she'd fought for months, but Sammie wouldn't allow her mind to go there today. She had too much to be thankful for and heaven knew, she'd cried enough for two lifetimes already.

Poking her head outside, she noted a trendy Southwestern restaurant a few steps down the street, a smoke shop, a fancy children's boutique and a little café with tables set for two outside the entrance. Warmth filled her chest and she whispered, "This is home now."

Yesterday, Tagg and Callie had insisted on picking her up from the airport and had driven her to her new apartment. Callie must have offered a dozen times for Sammie to stay with them at Worth Ranch, but Sammie would never impose on them. Callie was eight months pregnant and the expectant couple deserved to enjoy this very special time in their lives without a houseguest.

Upon Jackson's recommendation, Sammie had used an online service to find a furnished rental in a Spanish-style building with adobe archways and a red stone tiled garden patio. She'd sold everything she'd owned in Boston in a symbolic act meant to add closure to her old life. Only a few special pieces were salvaged from her father's meager estate. She'd placed in storage her father's favorite lounge chair, an antique grandfather clock that cuckooed on the hour and a few other items she couldn't bear to part with belonging to her parents.

"Welcome to Arizona, neighbor." She jumped at the sound and turned to find a man wearing a chef's apron approaching from the café. His broad smile creased the perfect planes of his olive-toned face. His voice held the slightest hint of a Spanish accent as each word was enunciated with emphasis when he spoke.

He came to stand before her and stretched out his hand in greeting. "I'm Sonny Estes. I own Sonny Side Up Café."

"Hello. I'm Sammie Gold. Great name, by the way." She slipped her hand in his grasp and he gave it one distinct shake, before releasing her. "Sonny Side Up, I mean. I noticed your storefront this morning."

"Thanks. You're putting a boot store in here, correct?"

Surprised, she inclined her head a little with curiosity. "That's right. How'd you know?"

"Jack's a friend of mine. And my landlord, but I forget that on occasion. Like when I crush him on the court."

She blinked and tried to picture the *GQ* cowboy in white shorts. "Tennis?"

His eyes crinkled with amusement. "No, no. Basketball."

"Oh." That made more sense to her for some reason.

"He told me you'd be coming by to see the place." He peered over her shoulder at the empty shop behind. "What do you think?"

"It's great. I mean it will be once I get my merchandise in here. I've got a pretty good idea already how I want this place to look."

"The location can't be beat. We get our share of local shoppers, but we also do well with tourists. Scottsdale is the Beverly Hills of Arizona.

She smiled. She'd heard that before. "All the better then."

"I'm glad Worth finally filled this spot. Not good for business, you know, to have empty shops on the boulevard."

"That's true."

"Stop by the café sometime and I'll buy you a meal." He winked and started walking backward. "I must get back to the kitchen. We usually pack the house at lunchtime."

Sammie waved goodbye to him and returned to the empty store, walking toward a back room that would serve as her office. She sat down on a neon green children's chair that was left behind, she presumed, when the space was called Kyra's Korner, a playland venue for small children. Jackson said the idea of an indoor babysitting activity center was sound, but it hadn't been situated in the right location. He had more faith in Boot Barrage.

The thought made her smile. Jackson liked boots. On women. Oh, who was she kidding? Jackson simply liked women, period. And they liked him back.

She leaned forward in the teensy seat, trying to forget about her little rendezvous with him in Vegas. The more she thought about it, the more she was glad she couldn't remember much of the night she spent in his bed. You can't long for what you can't remember. So, it was a good thing her memory of that night was virtually nonexistent.

The back door opened with a yawning sound and she spun her head to find Jackson stepping over the threshold. He bolted the door shut behind him and approached her with a laid-back smile. "Hey, Sammie."

"Oh, hi." She wished her breath wouldn't catch every time she set eyes on him. He was beautiful, no matter what expression he had on his face or what clothes he wore on his body, and there wasn't anything she could do about it. Today he had on jeans and a black jacket over a white cotton shirt. His hair, thick and rich as dark wheat, was covered with a tan felt hat. His eyes held a perpetual hint of mischief and were aimed at her calf-length boots.

He studied them, his eyes raking over the soft mocha leather straps and silver studs. She had her jeans tucked into them today, making her feel more like a Southwest woman than a Boston greenhorn.

He met her gaze. "Nice."

Self-conscious and a little flustered, she rose from the table to face him. "Thanks. I'm a walking advertisement for my boots."

"Who wouldn't stop to admire…*them,*" he asked as his gaze flowed over her legs, moved higher to touch on her breasts and then finally landed on her eyes.

Rattled, Sammie stammered, "I—I uh, didn't expect you this morning."

"It's almost lunchtime."

She shrugged. She wouldn't argue semantics with him. "Oh, I guess it is. I've been busy and didn't realize the time."

"Busy? Doing what?" Jackson scanned the room. "The place is empty."

"I know. I've been busy *thinking*…about what it'll look like when it's not empty."

"Can you put those thoughts down on paper?"

"I already have. I've worked on a draft. It's at my apartment."

"I'd like to see it, darlin'."

Sammie balked. "My apartment?"

"That *too,* but we have that dang pact, remember?"

How could she forget?

"I'm talking about the drafts. I've got a crew lined up to build the shelves and counter space and whatever else you decide you want. But I'd like to see your ideas first and go over them. Sound fair?"

Sammie had to get her head in the game. Jackson, obviously, didn't have a problem being around her, even if he teased her a bit, so she had to stop thinking of him as anything other than her very smart, very business-minded partner. "Yes, that sounds fair. I guess I didn't think you'd have much time to devote to Boot Barrage."

Jackson tipped his hat farther back on his head. "Seeing one of my enterprises get off to a good start is always smart business, Sammie. I invest not only my money, but also my time and ideas. So how about we shoot by your apartment, pick up your drafts and then discuss them over lunch?"

Lunch? With Jackson? She supposed there was no getting around spending time with him. He was successful and if he could show her how to make a go of her business in Scottsdale, she should be grateful. "Sure."

"One more thing," he said, taking her hand. The connection shot a jolt of heat straight through her system. He tugged her out the back door and into the parking lot. When she stared at him in question, he said with a dimpled smile, "This is for you."

"I've never driven an SUV before." With trepidation, Sammie sat behind the wheel of the Lincoln Navigator and coasted along the streets of Scottsdale. The new-car scent from the tan leather upholstery filled her nostrils as the shiny dashboard controls twinkled in the early afternoon sun. Everything surrounding her was rich and luxurious, including the man sitting in the passenger seat beside her.

"You're doing fine, Sammie," Jackson said nonchalantly, looking as if he hadn't a care in the world. The Navigator was the biggest car she'd ever driven. "You needed something with good storage space in back for boxes and samples. I figured a truck would be pushing it."

She gave him a sideways glance. "You figured right. Driving a truck would give me hives."

"It's not as hard as it looks."

"No, it's probably harder." She concentrated on the road and the newness of the controls. "I bet you've been driving your daddy's pickup truck since you were fifteen."

Jackson snickered. "More like thirteen, darlin'. My daddy didn't have a problem with his kids driving on their own property. He taught us the basics and let us have at it."

"It's a great car, Jackson." Sammie had to swallow past the lump in her throat. She'd been floored when Jackson told her the car was hers. She was overcome with gratitude but felt a little guilty; she doubted that Jackson was in the habit of giving cars to his business partners. He was doing a favor for Callie and Sammie was reaping the benefits. Sometimes it overwhelmed her, but at the same time, it made her all the more determined to make their business a success. Jackson's generosity wasn't something to sneeze it. "Tell me it's a business expense."

"It's yours. But on paper it's the Boot Barrage company car."

That rationale made her feel a little better. "Okay. I'll take good care of it."

They stopped by her apartment first, Jackson insisting on seeing the place. The set of his jaw and his reassuring look were enough to persuade her it wouldn't be a problem. It wasn't as if he was irresistibly drawn to her or anything. They could keep their hands off each other.

"I like it," he said, perusing the living space in the apartment. "Even if it's a snug fit."

She glanced at his jeans. *They* were a snug fit, but the apartment was adequate for her with two bedrooms, a living area and an efficient kitchen's worth of charm. "It's more than enough for me."

Sammie wouldn't show him the bedrooms but he took it upon himself to walk down the hallway and poke his head into both rooms anyway. Then, as she stood in the middle of the living room with the draft store plans in hand, he sauntered back over to her. "It has potential."

"It's a mess right now." Boxes of her clothes cluttered the floor at her feet. Photo frames and a set of dishes were stacked haphazardly on the kitchen counter. "I had a few things shipped from back East, but I'm mostly starting from scratch."

"You have a bed."

"Necessity of life, isn't it?"

"You got that right." His blue eyes darkened as he looked at her, and Sammie reminded herself that Jackson was a player. Flirting and teasing women were as natural to him as breathing. He wasn't a jerk about it either. He was a man who genuinely loved being with women. She couldn't fault him his killer looks and compelling charm.

Don't take him seriously, and you'll do fine, Sammie.

He bent down to flip open one box lid and raised his brows. "And boots."

She'd packed three large boxes of her own boots. "Another necessity of life."

He grinned. "Let's hope the women of Scottsale agree with you."

"I'm counting on it."

With a hand firmly on her back, Jackson led her toward the door. Before she locked up, Sammie glanced around at the textured walls and high arched doorways that accented the Southwestern flavor of the place and sighed.

"It'll feel like home before you know it," Jackson said, as if reading her mind.

This adventure was so new to her. She'd packed up her Boston apartment, leaving what was familiar to her completely behind. When she thought of it that way, shivers of apprehension rode up and down her spine. After all, she was an only child who'd lost her father and her business in the blink of an eye.

Now she fended off a full-fledged panic attack. She didn't want Jackson to see her moment of weakness. She'd moved three thousand miles away to a city with no coastline. It was a place foreign to her in most respects. But then, she thought about her best friend, Callie, and the rest of the Worths. They were her family now, Jackson included, and that notion made the knots in her stomach loosen. She bucked up her courage, giving herself a mental pep talk. She could do this and she would be successful. She smiled at Jackson as she turned the key in the lock. "I think so, too."

Jackson walked Sammie to her car, and juicy peaches sprang to mind. He figured since peach trees didn't grow in the desert, the sweet fragrance had to be coming from Sammie. "You smell delicious."

"It's my hand lotion. I put some on while we were in the apartment. It's kind of strong. If I'm making you hungry, I'm sorry."

There was hunger, and then there was hunger. Jackson glanced at the boots that hugged her calves. Even in a pair of jeans, with no leg showing, she turned him on. It was a damn shame.

Sammie was off-limits.

"Good thing we're going to lunch. I might have me some peach pie for dessert."

And it was a good thing he'd begun thinking straight again. He should have never laid a hand on Sammie. He'd been through the reasons in his mind a hundred times and had finally come to the conclusion that it wasn't only her boots that had appealed to him.

Right before she'd walked into that bar in Vegas, he'd learned that Blair Caulfield was coming back to Red Ridge.

Beautiful, rich, deceitful Blair Caulfield, the girl he'd once loved, was on her way to her hometown to cause havoc in the guise of tending to her ailing Aunt Muriel.

Jackson wanted to think he was over her, but one minute he was on the phone hearing the news of her return from a close friend and the next minute he was finding solace in the arms of the unsuspecting Sammie Gold.

In a way, Sammie had been just what he'd needed that night. To make him forget Blair and the heartache she'd caused him.

By the time Sammie had thrown her arms around his neck and kissed him, it was all the encouragement he'd needed. And making love to Sammie had been hot. But his lust for her had shocked him back to his senses the following morning. He'd had to do the right thing and set some boundaries.

"You're driving this time." Sammie's voice broke into his thoughts.

Before he could argue she climbed into the passenger seat and buckled up. She added, "I can get a better feel for the lay of the land this way. Without having to concentrate on the road."

She had a point. Jackson accepted her decision and settled behind the wheel. Sammie had been through a lot lately and she was trying to cope with all the changes in her life. He couldn't blame her for being gun-shy of driving in a town she didn't know in a powerhouse of a new car.

He set the drafts in her lap and started the engine. At least driving would keep his eyes on the road and not on her. When she had driven the Navigator earlier, he'd had freedom enough to look his fill. She was cute, with a slender frame and a pleasant face dotted with a few freckles across the bridge of her nose that she tried to cover up with makeup. But she wasn't even close to the kind of woman who usually attracted him. So why, he asked himself, was he drawn to her? "Do you like hot and spicy?" he asked.

Sammie stammered, "I, uh…" Then she turned in the seat to face him, her body at an angle and both brows digging into her forehead. "What exactly do you mean?"

Jackson grinned. He added innocence to her list of attributes. "Food, Sammie. I'm talking Cajun. There's this great place just outside of town."

"Oh." She was so dang relieved she might have melted into the upholstery as she sank back down in her seat. "That sounds fine."

It was refreshing to be with a guileless woman for a change, Jackson thought. Someone whose expression told you exactly what she was thinking. She wasn't coy or pretentious. It was a rare thing.

An hour later, Jackson spread out Sammie's drafts for Boot Barrage on the cleared restaurant table. They'd eaten chicken and rice and now sat beside each other sipping iced tea.

Sammie took a big gulp of hers. "Wow, my mouth's on fire."

"I thought you liked Cajun food."

Sammie gave him a sheepish look. "I've never tried it before. I'm not into spicy."

"Is that a fact," Jackson remarked, not allowing his mind to go wicked. "Why'd you agree to it then?"

She stared into his eyes. "I figured this is my year for firsts."

Her gaze darted to his mouth and lingered long enough to make his groin tighten. The sweet smell of peaches drifted to his nose again. "I mean…I don't usually venture too far from my comfort zone," she said.

"You don't?"

"No. My tastes aren't very adventurous."

"Maybe you should change that."

She shook her head and her short hair moved and then fell right back into place again. "There are enough changes in my life right now."

Jackson swallowed the last of his tea. "Are we still talking food here?"

Sammie hesitated, then lifted tentative eyes his way. "Uh, just so you know, I'm not the kind of girl…who *experiments* with food…just because it's available."

No. She wasn't talking about food. "I knew that about you."

"Good, because I don't think I'd try Cajun again…just for the record. Though, it's pretty on the plate and all."

Jackson hid a smile. They'd already decided this in Las Vegas. They had agreed not to sleep together again, but apparently Sammie had more to say on the subject. "Okay, no more Cajun food for you."

She smiled with relief and Jackson pointed to the paper laid out on the table, returning to the business at hand. "Now, about your designs…"

The next few days flew by. Sammie was busier than she'd been in her entire life. She'd made calls to her private boot venders and haggled over prices, set up a whole new Excel spreadsheet for taking inventory, ordered window dressings for the shop and interviewed for part-time help. At night she'd unpack her belongings at her apartment, do laundry and make herself a salad before collapsing into bed.

She'd been in touch with Jackson every day. He didn't disappoint on the business end of things. He wasn't lying about helping her get the new enterprise off the ground. What they needed was a good start and Jackson knew some tricks of the trade. He'd stopped by her apartment once to check on her progress, and this morning he'd beaten her in getting to the shop. She saw his king-cab Ford truck as she pulled into the small parking lot behind Boot Barrage.

She opened the back door and walked in on him as he measured a wall with a thick chrome tape measure. His back was to her and he didn't bother turning around. "Mornin'," he said over his shoulder. "The crew will be here in a few minutes. Thought I'd speak with the contractor before he gets started in here."

"Good morning," she said quietly. She closed the door behind her and tried not to gape at Jackson. He wore a snug cotton T-shirt that hugged his shoulders and a pair of faded blue jeans tight enough for images to flash through her mind of how good he'd looked in the raw.

He also had a leather tool belt wrapped around his waist. *A tool belt.* Really?

Sammie held back a sigh. Every time she saw him, she fell a little more in lust with him. But that was only because he was beautiful. Eye candy. A hunk.

"Okay, that's great. I can't wait until they get started on this place."

Jackson grunted in agreement and then went back to jotting down figures on a clipboard. He had arranged for a desk and chair from one of his offices to be delivered the other day. She'd set up her laptop on it and had worked here whenever she could.

"You coming to Callie and Tagg's for dinner tonight?" he asked, still concentrating on the figures he jotted down.

Her dear friend Callie had been patient with her. She'd invited her over every night this week, but Sammie had been too busy. She'd promised her that tonight would be the night—she'd missed her friend and they were both anxious to spend time together—but Sammie hadn't known that Jackson was invited, too.

"Yes, I'm going."

"No sense in both of us driving out there in separate cars," he said, studying another wall he was measuring. "I'll drive you to Red Ridge."

"Oh, no. That's not nec—"

Jackson turned to her and a jolt of new desire paraded through her stomach. He was every woman's fantasy, a blond-haired, blue-eyed tool-belt-wearing hunk of a man. Sammie had always prided herself on not being a shallow female *until* she'd met Jackson Worth. He was in a class all by himself as far as she was concerned. But she'd reminded herself a hundred times that business and pleasure didn't mix. Especially not for her.

Her creep of an ex-boyfriend, Allen Marksom, had driven that point home.

"Oh," she said, quickly realizing her mistake. "Callie asked you to drive me there."

"Carpooling saves the environment."

"Callie worries about me too much."

"She's your friend."

"But still, if you were only going on my account, you don't—"

"Two things, Sammie," he said in a serious tone. "I like spending time with my family. And I don't argue with pregnant ladies." He sent her a quick nod. "Just so you know."

She nodded back. "Got it."

When the crew showed up for work, she and Jackson went over the plans to make sure they were all on the same page. Excited, Sammie's mental picture of Boot Barrage was finally coming to fruition.

Her boot boutique would be unique, not only because of the exquisite boots she'd be selling, but also because she'd give them her personal touch and a guarantee of repair, restoration and quality. She'd been given a lifetime's worth of instruction by a high-end designer as to how to properly maintain and treat the boots to give them the longest life.

Each and every boot would come with the Gold Guarantee and that would be her selling point. Her own boots were testimony to personal care and longevity. She'd make sure her customers got the same level of quality.

"Once we get started you won't be able to come in here," the head contractor, Justin Cervantes, said. "Safety reasons."

Jackson nodded. "We figured as much. Not a problem."

"How long before we'll be able to get back in, exactly?" Sammie asked.

Mr. Cervantes scanned the space, doing mental calculations. "We've got to texture the walls, build the shelving, put in the counters and paint. Mr. Worth wants it done quickly. If we work steady through the weekend, I'd say not until midweek. That's as quick as we can do it." He sent a solid look to Jackson. "I'll be in touch every day."

"Sounds good to me," Jackson said.

His cell phone rang. He took a quick look at the screen and then excused himself to deal with the call.

Sammie finished the conversation with the contractor, thanking him and giving him her phone number also in case he had any questions about design. Exhilaration stirred in her belly. This was really happening. She'd have a new place, one that was infused with enough cash to give the establishment a good start. She was getting a second chance, doing something she loved to do. Back in Boston she'd had a little hole-in-the-wall boutique, hardly any space at all, yet she'd made a decent living and enjoyed some success. This space was three times the size. It would be luxurious and comfortable for her and her clients. She planned on spending most of her time here. Diving into her work with guns blazing would never be an issue.

When Jackson finished with his call, he motioned for

Sammie to meet him in the back room. The space would serve as her office and a lounge for her employees, and behind that area a stockroom would be built to house the inventory.

"What's up?" she said.

"That was my brother Clay. He's inviting us to a little show they're having at Penny's Song tomorrow night. Since we're both coming out to the ranch, he suggested that we stay with them for the weekend."

Penny's Song was a dude ranch on the Worth property designed for children recovering from illness. Sammie had been there once, when Callie had married Tagg. The charity helped provide children an easy way to acclimate back into society. Young Penny Martin, a local Red Ridge resident, had been the inspiration, and upon her death, all three Worth brothers had helped in starting up the foundation. The charity had touched the heart and soul of the entire town.

But the invitation to stay out at the ranch with Jackson brought a wave of fear to her heart. She'd hoped to keep as much distance from him as possible and it appeared that she was losing that battle.

A wealth of guilt glided through her mind. She hadn't out and out lied to Callie about her time spent with Jackson in Las Vegas, but when they'd talked, she'd skirted the issue and hid the truth from her. Something she'd never done before. Just being in the same room with Jackson and Callie would fray her nerves. She wasn't looking forward to it.

"I'm sure you've got plans for Saturday night." Sammie could only hope.

Jackson shook his head and gave a nonchalant shrug. "Actually, I'm open."

Great.

Why in heaven's name didn't he have a date or something?

Her cell phone rang this time. And she didn't have to look at the screen to know it was Callie. Small-town life was like that, she was finding out, and news traveled fast, especially in a close-knit family. Sammie knew exactly what Callie would say.

"You'll stay with us," Callie said a few seconds into the conversation, proving Sammie right. "At our house, and Jackson will stay with Clay."

"Callie, I love you dearly, but I don't want to impose on you and Tagg."

"You're not. I'd love some female company up here."

Tagg and Callie's house was set at the base of the Red Ridge mountains on the site of the original Worth house built in the 1800s. Clay and his family lived on a bigger piece of land that supported the cattle, corrals and outer buildings. All of it was considered Worth property. Tagg raised horses, and Clay raised cattle. And Jackson was the dealmaker and entrepreneur of the family.

"You'll stay the weekend. Come on…say you will. Please."

"Okay," Sammie said without pause. She couldn't disappoint her best friend. She'd just have to find a way to deal with being around Jackson twenty-four-seven.

Sammie had met steeper challenges before.

Though, for the life of her now she couldn't recall a single one.

Three

"Squeeee! I'm tickled to death you're here for the entire weekend." A very pregnant Callie had opened her front door and stepped out onto the porch before Sammie had gotten a chance to knock. Her friend wrapped her arms around Sammie as far as her baby bump would allow. Her bulging stomach took up a good foot and half of space between them. Callie called it "happy space."

Callie's eyes beamed and her face was radiant with a pregnancy glow.

Sammie grinned. The two had met and become friends while going to college in Boston. "Since when do you say things like 'tickled to death'?"

Callie laughed and her hearty laughter echoed in the vast open space surrounding them. Behind her stood the Red Ridge mountain range where Callie and Tagg had spoken their vows. "You know I grew up in Red Ridge. Back in Boston, we're *jazzed*. But here, we get tickled to death."

"Or tickled pink?"

Callie nodded. "That, too. You'll catch on. It won't be long until you're speaking our language out here in the wild, wild West. This weekend we'll be roomies again." Callie was beside herself with happiness. "Oh, I've missed you. I can't wait to have a good sit down and catch up on everything."

Behind Sammie's eyes, tears stung. Callie was the closest thing she had to a sister. Her gracious welcome touched something deep inside. She hadn't felt this kind of love since her father died. She'd lost her mother at an early age, so he and Sammie had been very close up until the day he'd taken his last breath. If she'd had any doubts about making the move to Arizona, they'd all just vanished into thin air. She'd made the right move. "I've missed you, too."

"The timing's good, too, isn't it?" Callie asked. "We're not pulling you and Jackson away from your work, right?"

Hearing her name paired with Jackson's gave her momentary palpitations, but she recovered quickly. She didn't want to walk on eggshells, worried that someone might guess they'd slept together. It was a secret she'd have to keep without experiencing a guilt trip every time Jackson's name was mentioned.

"It's absolutely good timing." It was the truth. She would be able to spend the weekend here and still have enough time to put the finishing touches on her apartment when she returned home. She was almost finished hanging pictures and organizing her kitchen. As for Boot Barrage, the crew wouldn't be done with construction for several days and Sammie didn't have any stock due to arrive until the end of the week.

She glanced at Tagg, who'd gone out to the car to say hello to Jackson. The two men were deep in conversation as Jackson pulled Sammie's small suitcase out of his truck.

He turned and found her watching him, and that ridiculous jolt smacked her right between the eyes again.

He studied her for a second, his gaze drifting down to her black ankle boots with three-inch heels and Grecian straps crisscrossing her calves. The boots complemented the flower-print black and white dress she wore. The only jewelry she wore was a lacy silver necklace that dipped over her breasts with earrings that matched.

It was as if Jackson hadn't noticed anything else on her body but her boots. And now his gaze slowly rose up her legs, over her little dress, until he looked her straight in the eye.

The moment froze in time.

Her nerves jumped.

Get a grip, Sammie.

She had a feeling she'd be saying that to herself a hundred times before this weekend was over. She could endure Jackson's hot looks and the momentary weakness she lapsed into when she gazed at him, if only Tagg and Callie wouldn't find out the truth. She vowed to get over this crazy thing she had for Jackson. Somehow.

Sammie was the first to break eye contact.

Callie grabbed her hand. "Come inside. I want to show you the nursery. Tagg's got it all set up."

"I can't wait to see it. I've been trying to picture it in my head from your descriptions."

"I've been boring everyone I know about it. But trust me, seeing is believing and I think you're going to like it. It's a combination of what Tagg and I love most."

"That's intriguing."

They walked down the hallway, and the subtle baby-powdery scent of fresh diapers and all things infant wafted by. She followed Callie into the sunny room.

Sammie took one step inside and was transported to a

Western rodeo, baby-style. The walls were the faintest beige with accents of browns and blues. One part of the longest wall was painted with sweet little lambs, goats and chicks in a white picket pen as part of the petting arena. The other side of the wall was a mural of a rodeo stadium, the shoots filled with friendly looking bulls and beautiful black stallions. A replica of a shiny silver championship buckle took center stage directly over the crib with the name Rory Worth scrolled in italic lettering on it.

Sammie's mouth gaped open. "Callie, this is gorgeous." The whole thing was tastefully done and so sweet. Perfect for a Worth baby boy. "It's the Superbowl of baby nurseries."

"Thank you. We're pretty happy with how it turned out."

"I've never seen anything like this. You thought this up?"

"Yes, it was my idea, but with input from Tagg, of course. We had fun picking out the furniture for the room. But I can't take credit for painting the mural. That was created by an artist. Now that it's all done, I can't wait for the baby to arrive." Callie patted her belly and her eyes grew wide with delight. "Oh, he just kicked. Here." Callie grabbed Sammie's hand and put it over her stomach.

The skin rippled under her palm and Sammie's hand moved from the motion. "Oh, wow." She took a swallow, awed at feeling the life move inside Callie. Softly, she said, "This little guy is ready to ride broncos."

"I know. He's very active and keeps me up most nights. He's a little kicker."

"I can see that." Sammie hadn't given up on the idea of having children. She wanted them one day, but that day seemed to be postponed further and further into her future. It was a timeline without end and Sammie had to resign herself to that for now. She could only focus on making a home in Arizona and building a business. Babies might come later down the road, or not at all. That notion pulled at her heart with sadness and she hurried the thought away. "The baby's strong and healthy, Callie."

"I think so, too. I'm trying to do all the right things for him."

"I know you are. You're daddy didn't raise a slacker."

Callie's bright smile dimmed a little. "No, he didn't."

Instantly Sammie realized her blunder. Just months ago, Callie had been torn between her love for Tagg and her father, Hawk Sullivan. The two men were bitter business rivals; they hated each other. "Sorry to bring up a sore subject."

"No it's okay. It's the same old, same old with my dad. But I think he is softening a little. I'm hoping that once the baby comes, my father will see the error of his ways and want to be a part of our lives."

"And Tagg is good with that?"

"Tagg? I'm beginning to think he's more reasonable about it. He trusts my judgment when it comes to my father. Having Tagg's trust means everything to me. I won't abuse it. My husband knows our baby comes first, no matter what."

"That's a good thing, Callie. You and Tagg have come a long way." The baby gave another kick and roll. Sammie smoothed her hand over the baby bump tenderly before pulling away. "You've got a good life here, my friend."

"I do." She sighed. "Once Tagg and I worked out the kinks, we ended up with something pretty special."

Sammie stared into Callie's eyes. They radiated encouragement and kindness. Callie didn't have to say that she hoped Sammie would find the same happiness. Sammie read it all in her sincere expression.

"Come into the kitchen while I fix supper. You can tell me all about Boot Barrage. I'm anxious to hear everything. Don't leave a crumb out."

"Okay, okay. I will, but you have to stop saying things like 'don't leave a crumb out,' or I won't recognize you anymore."

Callie only smiled as she led Sammie into the kitchen.

"How's our little Rodeo Rory doing today?" Jackson asked, coming to stand beside Callie as she chopped cucumbers for the salad. He gave her a peck on the cheek.

Callie turned from the kitchen counter to face him, her lips forming a perfectly adorable pout. "Stop calling him that and we'll be fine."

Sammie chopped tomatoes as she listened to their banter.

"Tagg's paying me to call him that," Jackson said in his own defense.

"I'll pay you more not to," Callie said.

"How much more?"

Callie gave Sammie a sideways glance and clucked her tongue. "Can you believe this guy? Negotiating about his soon-to-be godchild?"

"It's pretty low down, if you ask me," Sammie said, tsking and shaking her head. "I would never do such a thing. Rory will know just which godparent has his back."

Jackson cut her a glance with raised brows and a twinkle of admiration in his eyes. Sammie was a fast learner. She had to be to keep up with the Worths.

Jackson stole a slice of cucumber from the pile of chopped vegetables, plopped it into his mouth and stepped back before Callie could swat his hand away. "Hey, blame Tagg, not me."

Tagg appeared at that moment, leaning against the kitchen doorjamb, arms folded, his gaze faithfully on Callie. The Worth men were deadly handsome and when they looked at a woman the way Tagg looked at his wife, it was pure heaven. Sammie sighed quietly.

"Leave me outta this, bro. I have to live here, remember?" Tagg said.

"So does Rory. Poor kid. He'll be in high school and dreaming of baby lambs and goats." Jackson was pretty pleased with himself at that comeback. Callie simply shook her head.

"Maybe he'll dream of riding Razor the bull and winning a championship buckle." Tagg sauntered into the room.

"Now that's a nightmare waiting to happen." Callie tossed lettuce into a bowl and Sammie dumped the tomato wedges in. The two of them worked hand in hand just like when they were roommates in college. "Don't you go putting bull riding thoughts into our son's head."

"Me? Not a chance." Tagg sidled up next to Callie and wrapped his arm around her rotund waist. "Honey, you know that boy's gonna bust broncos. Maybe even break a few of my stallions here at the ranch."

Callie nibbled on her lower lip and stared into Tagg's eyes with so much love Sammie could have melted. "Oh, yeah. That's right. I forgot," Callie said and gave a quick shake of the head to Sammie, as if to say that's never going to happen.

Sammie chuckled, Jackson grinned and Tagg kissed Callie once again, right before she announced, "Dinner's ready. Tagg, would you help me serve while Jackson and Sammie get settled in the dining room?"

"Oh, I'll help you serve." Sammie took a stance by the stove and picked up the oven mitts, giving Tagg no choice but to retreat when she glanced at him. "I'd love to. It'll be just like old times."

"Sounds good to me," Tagg said amiably, grabbing two beers out of the refrigerator. He tossed one underhanded to Jackson, who caught it without flourish.

"I have eight months of pampering my friend to catch up on," Sammie said to Callie. "Starting right now."

Callie smiled. "I've been getting my fair share of pampering."

"But not from me."

Not only did she want to help Callie and feel like a part of this family, but the less time she spent alone with Jackson, the better. It was a win-win.

Until the men walked out of the room and Callie asked, "So, you and Jackson seem to be getting along well."

Sammie concentrated on pulling the roast out of the oven. She knew this conversation was coming whether she wanted it or not. It was only natural for Callie to be curious about the two of them. With potholders secure on both hands, Sammie pulled down the oven door and lifted the roasting pan onto a cooling rack. "Yeah, we are."

"He's got a good head for business. With your smarts and his backing, you'll both do well with Boot Barrage."

"Thank you," Sammie said cautiously, trying not to prolong the conversation. She didn't want to lie to Callie. Sins of omission were bad enough.

"I mean, Jackson's a good guy and all and he'll make a great partner."

"Uh-huh." Sammie lifted aluminum foil off the roast and steam shot straight up in the air. She waved at it with her potholder. The pungent scent of onions, herb seasonings and brisket filled the room. "This looks delicious."

"It's Jackson's favorite. My brother-in-law gets a bad rap sometimes, but he's really good-hearted."

Callie wouldn't let it rest, so Sammie felt obligated to add to the conversation. "Well, I know one thing for sure— I wouldn't have a business if it wasn't for the two of you. I owe both of you."

"You've thanked me enough, Sammie. You don't owe anyone anything. And if Jackson didn't think you had a shot here in Arizona, I doubt he would have gone into business with you."

"Oh, yeah? I thought it was your arm twisting that finally convinced him."

Callie had the good grace to laugh. "That, too. He doesn't mess with pregnant ladies. At least he's said so a dozen times. I pretty much have carte blanche with him." She covered a basket of thickly sliced bread with a red paisley napkin and finished assembling the salad. "I've come to love Jackson like a brother actually, and you know how much I care about you. I figured you two could work together without a problem."

Sammie's brows furrowed and curiosity got the best of her. "What kind of problem?"

Callie tilted her head to the side and picked up the bread basket. "The you're-too-smart-to-get-involved-with-him kind of problem."

"Oh, that." Sammie refrained from saying more. Callie handed her a large fork and knife and Sammie focused on slicing the roast.

Callie continued, "He's gorgeous to look at and has a devil's worth of charm, but he's—"

"Not my type." Sammie rationalized that her admission wasn't a lie. Jackson was so out of her league it was laughable.

Callie blew out a breath. "I'm glad to hear that. Jackson's intentions are good, and he never sets out to hurt anyone, but he's pretty much a heartbreaker. It all has to do with some girl he was crazy about in high school—Blair Caulfield. Ever since she left him when he was seventeen Jackson has had commitment phobia. He's never had a long-term relationship. Women love him though. I mean, what's not to love? But he's never wanted to settle down with anyone.

So any woman that gets serious about him stands to be disappointed."

What happened in the past between her and Jackson was done and there was no going back to change things. Heck, she couldn't remember the good parts of that night anyway. And even as guilt wormed its way into her stomach, she had to reassure Callie that all would be well. "If you're warning me about Jackson, you don't have to. I get it."

Sammie was dying to know what had happened between Jackson and Blair, but now wasn't the time to delve into it.

"It's just for your own good, honey. After what happened with that loser Allen and, uh…"

"Losing my father." Sammie finished her sentence so her sensitive friend wouldn't feel uncomfortable bringing it up. The pain of her dad's death was buried deep in her heart. Sammie struggled each and every day not to think about how much she missed him. And when she did think of him, she tried to remember the happier times, before he'd taken ill.

"Yes, after losing your father. I'd hate to see you get hurt again. After all, you're part of the family now."

Sammie released her uneasy feelings. Being accepted as a member of Callie's family was what she really wanted. Hearing her say it put a glow in her heart. "I am?"

Callie nodded. "Yes, of course you are. Let's go serve those hungry Worth men. They get grouchy when they're not fed." Sammie and Callie picked up their dishes and brought them into the dining room.

"C'mon you two, get up and dance."

Callie's plea made Jackson chuckle. He took his gaze off his sister-in-law to glance at Sammie and then shook his head. The last time he'd danced with the slender brunette they'd ended up in bed together. "No, thanks. I think Tagg and I will just sit here and watch the show." Jackson leaned back on the parlor sofa and stretched out his legs.

"You've got yourself a better dance partner than me now, sweetheart," Tagg added.

Callie laid a hand on her belly and swung her body to the country music sounds echoing in the room. "I think you've got a point, honey. Sammie and I rocked back in college." The girls gave each other a nod in agreement.

Clayton Worth's youthful baritone voice rang out from the stereo. Callie loved Clay's music. He'd been a teenage superstar and had since retired from singing to run Worth Ranch. His songs were now considered classic country and every one of his fans knew all the words, Sammie and Callie included.

The women stood in front of the fireplace with glasses of sparkling cider in hand and swayed their hips to the beat.

"If this helps get Rory settled down, good godmother that I am, I'm happy to do it. Like I said earlier, the baby will know which godparent he can count on." Sammie had mischief in her eyes as she aimed her comment at Jackson.

"You think you're cute, don't you?" he asked.

Sammie shrugged and sipped her drink as she swayed back and forth. Trouble was, she *was* cute, shimmying to the music in her little summer dress. Jackson slid his gaze down her legs and cursed silently at the vision she made in high-heel ankle boots.

"She is more than cute," Callie said, sticking up for her best friend. "And she rocks on the dance floor. Oh, the baby's loving this right now. And it feels pretty good not having him punch my stomach. I think the boy wants out."

Jackson sipped his red wine. It was getting harder and harder to watch Sammie make those dance moves with her body swinging and swaying effortlessly. She and Callie were having innocent fun, rocking the baby and enjoying the music, but it was still damn tricky keeping his eyes off her.

His mind slid back to the night when he'd made love to her. Her skin had been firm but soft under his palms as he ran his hands up and down her body. Her breasts were small but perfectly round, and he'd filled his hands and then his mouth, drinking her in. He'd been hot and hungry for her when he finally did the deed, and she didn't disappoint. His groin pulsed at the memory.

"Something wrong?" Tagg asked in a low voice, watching him carefully. "You've got drool on your lips."

Jackson snapped his head away from the women who had danced their way over to the window out of earshot. He pressed the back of his hand to his mouth and wiped at it. "Don't worry. Nothing's there."

"You're sure?" Tagg's concerned expression wore on his nerves. "I've seen that look on your face before."

"There's no look, Tagg. And if there was one, it'd be none of your business."

"But there isn't one, right?"

Jackson kept annoyance out of his tone, barely. "That's what I said."

"Okay." Tagg grabbed the bottle of wine and refilled their glasses.

"What are you two whispering about over there?" Callie asked as she and Sammie danced over to the sofa just as the song ended.

"I was about to ask Jackson if he'd made any headway on the land he's been itching to get his hands on."

"Oh, right. How's that coming?" Callie asked.

"Not good," Jackson said. He slid over on the sofa so both women could take a seat. Callie sat next to Tagg, which left no place for Sammie to sit but practically on his lap. "I found out yesterday who owns the land."

"What land?" Sammie asked with eyes keenly interested and her face flushed from dancing.

"It's land that Jackson's been wanting to add to the Worth property. Tell her about it, Jackson," Callie said.

Jackson leaned back, giving himself a little space from Sammie. Her sweet scent radiated straight into his nostrils, but he managed to focus on his explanation. "It goes way back to the time when Worth Ranch was just getting its start. There's a pretty piece of land on the other side of Elizabeth Lake that we don't own. My father tried and tried for years to secure that land. It's part of Worth history but the owner of that strip of land would never sell."

"Why not?" Sammie asked.

"He's a stubborn old coot, claiming what's his is his and no amount of money was going to make him sell his property."

Tagg added, "We don't want anyone to develop on that land."

"And someone's trying to do that?" Sammie asked.

"Well...yeah," Jackson said. "There's been rumors for years that a real estate developer wants to put low-cost housing in right by the lake. Nothing ever came of it, but now things have changed."

"How so?" Sammie asked.

Jackson's lips twisted. "Because old Pearson Weaver finally sold the land out from under my nose. The old codger wouldn't even give me a chance to bid on it. And the person who bought the land has come back to town. With an agenda."

Tagg's brows dented into his forehead. "So, who bought the land?"

Jackson told himself that he'd gotten over her. He hadn't laid eyes on her since she left town more than fourteen years ago, even though he'd heard that she'd been back to visit her aunt Muriel a couple times in between husbands.

But first loves, whether good or bad, stick with you. Now she had the land his family wanted and was here in Red Ridge. He hated thinking about her, much less saying her name out loud. "Blair Caulfield."

Four

Sammie spent the next morning with her best friend and enjoyed every single minute catching her up on news. She'd told her about her plans for Boot Barrage and how her new apartment was coming along. She'd talked about her loser boyfriend, the rat, and how he'd stolen her money and her heart. He'd been a con artist—she even doubted whether Allen Marksom had been his real name. She'd fallen for his supposedly kind nature and the attention he'd paid her, when all the while he'd been planning to bamboozle her and take off with her operating cash. She felt sorry for the next woman he would victimize. She'd given the police all the details about him and hoped that one day he'd get his sticky fingers caught in a vice.

Now Sammie leaned against the corral fence watching Ruby, a feisty mare named not only because of her reddish coat but also after the legend of the Worth ruby necklace going back to the founding of ranch.

Family and history were important to the Worths, and Sammie was beginning to see just how much. And she couldn't help but wonder about Jackson and Blair Caulfield. Jackson rarely showed any side of himself that wasn't in control. He usually didn't let too much of anything rattle him. But he'd seemed truly upset when he'd mentioned Blair's name yesterday. Was it the fact that she'd snatched the land out from under him that troubled him, or was it that Blair had returned to Red Ridge and was only miles away from him now? Sammie wondered if he could still love a woman who had broken his heart, hurt his pride and scarred him for life.

"Where's Callie?"

The sound of Jackson's voice made her jump. She turned to find him approaching, the initial sight of him making her breath catch.

"Thought you two would be thick as thieves today."

"We always are—don't you doubt it for a second—but she's resting right now. We're going shopping in Red Ridge later."

Jackson leaned against the corral fence and watched the horses in the pen. Ruby nudged Callie's palomino, Freedom, and they snorted quietly as they faced off.

"Oh, yeah? For anything special?"

"Nope. Us womenfolk don't need a reason to shop."

He turned to see her caustic grin and then shook his head. "You're not as sweet as you look, Sammie Gold."

"Gawd, I hope not." She shuddered at the thought. "Because I've been told I look about fifteen."

"Did you thank them for the compliment?"

Sammie's mouth formed an O, and she shook her head. "No. Wish I'd have thought of that at the time."

"And you don't look fifteen." Jackson raked his gaze over her with leisure, as if he had the perfect right to. She felt as though she'd been stripped naked. Which she had been, but that was another matter. Jackson drew a sharp breath. "Not even a little."

What was he doing here anyway? He was supposed to be staying over at the main house with Clay and Trish. But this was Worth land and she couldn't really tell him to go away. Besides, after she got over her first jolt of mind-blowing lust, she kind of liked having him around. He was her guilty pleasure and she was experiencing a lot of guilt lately. Something about Jackson pulled at her and made her take uncharacteristic chances.

"But, according to you, I'm not so cute and I'm not so sweet. Makes a girl wonder what she really is."

"Fishing for a compliment, Sammie?" Jackson asked with a crooked but deadly smile.

Sammie inclined her head and told the truth. "Maybe."

Jackson glanced at her blue jeans fitted neatly into latte-colored midcalf boots. He took a swallow and his gaze narrowed when it returned to touch her eyes. "If I told you the truth, then I'd have to kill you."

She stared at him, trapped by the warmth in his eyes. She spoke softly on a shallow breath, "If that's not a gutless way to get out of it, I don't know what is."

"It's not gutless, Sammie. I don't take just any woman to bed," he said. "It might surprise you, but I use a lot of discretion."

"Which means you made an exception with me," Sammie blurted.

"No. It wasn't like that and you know it."

Sammie didn't want to talk about this ever again; they'd made their pact in Las Vegas. Yet she couldn't seem to stop herself. "What I know is that I came on to you that night. But can you blame a girl? If you were medication, you'd be the Super Sexy Pill for Women in Need."

A tick twitched in Jackson's jaw. "I'd like to think I'm a little more than that."

Oh, crap. Now she'd blown it. Most men would've taken her honest admission as a compliment. But Jackson was probably sick and tired of women coming on to him and he'd expected more from her than that. She should have been a bit more sensitive to his feelings. It wasn't his fault that he was every woman's dream man. "Jackson, I'm sorry. That came out wrong. I know you're a lot more than—"

He put up a stopping hand. "Look, for the record, while you might not believe this, I find you *cute, sweet* and a lot of fun. I was hot for you that night, Sammie. It was mutual. And if circumstances were different—" He paused and glanced down at her boots. Self-conscious, she shuffled her feet and then crossed her ankles.

"What?" She drew a sharp breath. If circumstances were different, he'd want to have a fling with her? A short-term affair? She was dying to know what he was thinking.

"Hell, this is awkward," he finally said.

"Tell me about it."

He lifted his head, pressed his lips tight and stared into her eyes. "I don't want to hurt you…that's for damn sure. I start getting antsy the minute a woman wants me to meet her family. Or shop for furniture or take a long vacation together. It's not in me to get serious. I don't do…permanent. I leave the happily-ever-after stuff to my brothers."

Technically, meeting her family wasn't an issue—she had none left. She had all the furniture she needed and there wasn't a long trip planned in her future. She was going to be rooted in Red Ridge for a long time. But she knew what Jackson was getting at. It was what Callie had tried to tell her yesterday.

Slim-hipped, slender, short-haired Sammie was stunned enough, learning that Jackson found her *hot* and desirable.

At least that night he had. It was almost better for her thinking the opposite was true, that he didn't find her attractive at all.

"Hey, you two," Tagg's deep voice carried across the yard.

They both snapped their heads toward him as he approached.

Sammie took a discreet step away from Jackson. Tagg darted a questioning glance at Jackson and then at her. Sammie gave him a big smile. "Hi, Tagg."

Jackson chimed in. "You ready for our ride?"

Tagg nodded. "Sure am. Been a while since we've saddled up together." He turned to Sammie. "I'd invite you to ride along, but Callie's up and chomping at the bit to go shopping. Seems there's one baby outfit in town she hasn't bought yet."

Sammie laughed. "Hey, I heard you're just as bad."

Tagg smiled. "Almost. I do my fair share, that's for darn sure. You two looked deep in conversation. Did I interrupt some important business you were conducting?"

"Nope, nothing important. Just jawing about the weather." Jackson kept his eyes on Tagg until he nodded. "And waiting on you. You ready to get going?"

"Yep. I'll take Wild Blue out. You can take Callie's mare, Freedom. She's been lonely since she stopped riding her."

"I'll do my best to accommodate the lady," Jackson said.

Tagg twitched his lips. "That *is* your specialty."

Jackson let the comment drop but not before he sent his brother a sour look. "See ya later, Sammie." He tipped his hat.

"Tell my wife to leave some things in Red Ridge for the rest of the shoppers," Tagg said with a wink.

Sammie chuckled. "I'll be sure to tell her. Have a nice ride."

The men walked toward the barn and Sammie headed for the house, looking forward to shopping in town with her best friend. She was eternally grateful she'd have a reprieve from spending the afternoon with Jackson.

It was bad enough she'd have to spend the entire evening with him.

"I love what you all have done with Penny's Song." Sammie looked around the little ranch bustling with life. She'd been here before but she'd never witnessed the place in action. Children of varying ages wearing western gear along with the "foremen volunteers" all seemed to jell together with symmetry of movement. Day had ebbed to a pink-hued dusk that settled on the land and added to the smooth rhythmic fluidity.

"It's really Clay and Trish's creation. Tagg, Callie and I lent a hand whenever we could," Jackson said.

The four of them walked into the center of the yard to meet up with Trish and Clay and their adopted baby daughter. "Welcome, you all," Trish said, holding the baby in her arms.

Jackson introduced her. "Trish, this is Sammie Gold."

"Sammie, it's nice to finally meet you. And congratulations on starting your boot business. I'm a fan. I've taken to wearing boots most of the time."

"Then we'll have a lot to talk about," Sammie said before turning toward the blond-haired baby. Apple-cheeked with eyes as clear blue as lake water, the baby studied Sammie's face. "She's precious."

"Thank you. We think so. This is Meggie."

Sammie smiled. "Hi, Meggie."

Jackson stroked the baby's head gently. "How's our girl today?" He leaned over and placed a tender kiss on her cheek. The softness in his tone surprised Sammie, and something snapped inside. She didn't want to see cool operator Jackson Worth's tender side. Enough was enough.

"Doing fine, Uncle Jackson," Trish said.

Jackson kept his eyes on Meggie and gave her a little lecture. "Remember, no boyfriends until you're in college."

Clay snorted. "More like when she's thirty and that's only if I like the guy."

Jackson grinned. "You're such a dad."

Clay's chest puffed out. "I know. It's pretty darn good. You should try it one day."

Jackson shook his head. "I've got Meggie and Rory to spoil. That'll keep me busy. Which reminds me," he said, placing his hand in his shirt pocket and coming out with a tiny teal box. "I picked this up for Meggie."

He handed the gift to Trish. "Would you do the honors?"

"You got Meggie another present?" Surprised, Trish's voice also held a note of gratitude.

He shrugged. "Isn't that what uncles are for?"

Trish peered at the box; Sammie was equally curious about the gift. "You're a fabulous uncle but not because you give Meggie gifts," Trish said.

"But it doesn't hurt. I'm hedging my bets. I wanna be the favorite uncle."

Trish shook her head at his nonsense and opened the box, finding a beautiful gold baby's bracelet inside. Trish fiddled with the teensy clasp and slipped the bangle over Meggie's wrist. She managed with Clay's help to fasten it. "It's beautiful, Jackson." Trish stood on tiptoes to kiss him on the cheek. "Thank you."

"Yeah, thank you," Clay said.

Sammie looked at Jackson and for a split second their eyes met. His were filled with love for baby Meggie, and an unfair knock pounded against her chest.

She vowed to steer clear of him for the rest of the night. But as fate would have it Clay wanted to introduce her and Jackson to the dozen children attending Penny's Song for the week. They walked the grounds together, meeting the boys and girls and many of their parents. They were mistaken for a married couple several times and Sammie was only too happy to allow Jackson to clear up the misunderstanding. Of course, he did it with ease and natural charm.

The scent of Jackson's woodsy cologne drifted her way and from time to time their shoulders would brush as they bent down to speak with a child. Sammie would tense up and pretend that she hadn't been rattled.

Yet all she'd felt had been eclipsed by the beauty of spirit that was Penny's Song. The Worth family had put their heart and soul into this project. Its success was an added bonus and proof positive of the generosity and kindness bred in all the Worths. Sammie felt immense pride in being treated like a part of the family, even more so after witnessing the good that Penny's Song was doing for the children.

When it came time to watch the evening's performance, she sat down on one of the long wooden bleachers, sliding in toward the middle. Tagg sat next to her and, because Callie needed to be on the aisle to stretch out her legs, Jackson wound around to the other side of the bench to slide in beside Sammie.

Sammie nibbled on her lower lip, fearing it would always be this way: Tagg with Callie, Clay with Trish and Sammie paired inadvertently with Jackson because they were the odd men out, so to speak. At least until one of them found a significant other.

Sammie couldn't imagine that for herself. She clearly wasn't shopping around for a boyfriend—she didn't have a spare minute to meet a good man. And Jackson had just given her a lecture about how he didn't "do permanent." She doubted he brought any women here to Penny's Song.

"It's a good night for a show. Weather's holding." Jackson laid his arm across the railing behind her, stretching out.

It was an innocent gesture as he awaited the performance, but as Sammie's body drifted backward and her short hair brushed his arm, she stiffened up.

"Relax, Sammie," Jackson said.

"I am relaxed," she said through gritted teeth.

He chuckled quietly. Darn him.

Sammie made a point of ignoring Jackson from then on, speaking to Callie until the show began. The children's performances ranged from campfire songs to rap, from ballet attempts to skits acted out by the older children. Sammie was awed and thoroughly entertained by the amateur talent show, even though there were a few hiccups like when the spotlights went out. Jackson and Clay raced to the rescue. And one other time a little girl got stage fright and started crying. It broke Sammie's heart to see the big tears fall on such a small fragile face and just before her parents would have intervened, a teenaged girl named Joanna sidled up next to her, held the child's hand and encouraged her to sing with her.

Jackson received a phone call and excused himself after the show concluded. Sammie walked toward the parked cars with the other Worths. "The kids were fabulous," Sammie said to Clay and Trish. "Thank you for the invitation. I can see you've put a lot of yourselves into this facility."

"Aside from raising Meggie, it's our crowning achievement here on the ranch," Clay said.

"You've done a great job on both accounts," Sammie said. "Meggie will have a wonderful environment to grow up around."

Trish smiled with Meggie sound asleep in her arms. "Yes, that's an added bonus." She kissed the top of the baby's head.

"Sammie." She turned around at the severe tone of Jackson's voice. He was taking long strides to catch up with them at the small unpaved parking lot.

"Is something wrong?" she asked.

"Don't panic, okay?"

Her heart leapt in her chest. How many times had she heard that in her lifetime? And each time it had definitely been cause for panic.

Don't panic...your father's dying.

Don't panic...your boyfriend stole your life's earnings.

"I can't promise you I won't. What's wrong, Jackson?"

Jackson winced. His eyes narrowed and his face twisted as if he didn't want to deliver the news. Then after taking a deep breath, he looked her straight in the eyes. "I just got off the phone with Justin. There was a fire at the shop. They'd been working all evening and it just happened. The fire department was called in. Justin blamed it on the wiring. Their equipment sparked, and the place caught fire."

Sammie's heart dropped. "Oh, no. Was anyone hurt?"

Jackson's expression eased. "No. That's the good news. But I should get over there. If you want to stay here with Callie—"

"No. I want to go with you. I should see what we're up against."

Jackson nodded. "Okay. I figured as much."

They quickly bid everyone farewell, went back to the ranch houses and packed up their belongings and got on the road. The long drive back to Scottsdale was silent for the most part except when Jackson tried to reassure her now and then that all would be well.

But even with Jackson's voice of reason, Sammie couldn't put aside the sense of dread that worked through her system. She prayed that this wasn't a *don't panic* scenario that wouldn't end, well, like all the other times before.

When Jackson and Sammie arrived at the shop, the fire department was already gone and Justin's crew had boarded up the front window that had blown out. The walls on the left side of the building were skeletal remains, and the renovation work the crew had already done was also ruined.

Jackson cursed when he first caught sight of the structure.

Sammie's throat closed. It was hard to look at. Her vision of Boot Barrage lay in a pile of ashes. A repugnant scent of destruction filled the air. Smoke coated the area in a murky haze and caused Sammie's eyes to burn. She was near tears already so the stinging sensation was even more difficult to battle, but at least she had a good excuse for the moisture running down her cheeks.

"Okay. Okay," Jackson said scanning the destruction with sharp eyes. "We can deal with this."

He took the tissue from her hand and dabbed at her misty tears. "Don't cry."

"Trying not to." She sniffed again, trying to find the strength to hold it all together. "But it's such a mess."

"Hey," Jackson said softly. "There's nothing here that can't be repaired or rebuilt."

"Really?"

"Justin said as much."

"It's going to be expensive."

"Yeah," Jackson said, dabbing at her eyes again.

She nodded. "It could have been worse," she said, her voice small. "No one was injured. And we're insured, right?"

Jackson smiled. "Yes, we're insured."

Sammie already knew that, but it was comforting to hear it from Jackson. Of course, if the wiring was at fault then there would be issues, but Sammie would leave that problem for another day.

"The crew will do the cleanup tomorrow and it should only set us back a short while, Sammie. Not the end of the world."

"No, not the end of the world," she agreed softly. Every

time she took a step forward, she felt as though she was being pulled two steps back.

"We'll postpone our grand opening for a couple of weeks. No big deal."

Sammie had forgotten about their grand opening. "Oh, right. I've already started on the promotion for it. I'm having flyers made and running an ad in the newspaper."

"So, we'll make a few changes."

She nodded, still feeling dreadful.

Jackson heaved a big sigh. "We should get out of here. The smoke's pretty thick. I could use a drink. You got any alcohol at your place?"

Under normal circumstances, Sammie wouldn't tempt fate by agreeing to have drinks with Jackson in the privacy of her apartment. The last time they were alone and alcohol had been involved, she'd wound up in his bed. But tonight Sammie really needed a friend and Jackson had pretty sturdy shoulders to lean on. She thought about what she had back at her apartment. "Wine."

"Thank you. I'd love some."

Jackson took Sammie by the hand and led her out of the building. They'd deal with Justin, the fire department and the insurance company tomorrow. Tonight, a glass of bold red merlot was in order.

Sammie felt slightly better by the time they reached her apartment. She'd only been in Arizona a short while, but each time she entered her place, it seemed more and more like home. "Have a seat," she said. "You can leave the luggage in here."

Jackson set her bag down and didn't take a seat. He followed her to the kitchen and leaned his back against the counter, watching her.

She grabbed a three-year-old bottle of red wine off a shelf next to the pantry and fished around inside a drawer for a corkscrew. Jackson approached, taking the corkscrew from her hand. "Allow me," he said.

She handed over the bottle too and reached into a cabinet for a wineglass.

He made quick work of opening the bottle and then raised a brow as he looked at the single glass on the counter. "You're not drinking wine?"

Sammie lifted the bottle and poured the wine. "No." She handed him the glass and moved away from him. Mixing wine and Jackson Worth was not an option.

"That's ridiculous," he said, grabbing another wineglass from the cabinet and pouring her half a glass. "I don't want to drink alone."

Sammie opened her mouth to say something, then thought better of it. She could certainly have a sip or two of wine with Jackson without fear of losing her mind and falling into bed with him.

When she hesitated to pick up the glass he offered, he pursed his lips. "We have a pact, remember?"

She whipped the glass out of his hand, frustrated with herself. "Okay. I know I'm being ridiculous."

Jackson's lips lifted into one of his killer smiles. "Thatta girl."

"Have a seat," she said, ignoring his charm and trying hard to forget about how tenderly he'd wiped her tears at the scene of the fire. How he made everything better.

He sat on a big upholstered chair and Sammie sat at an angle from him on the sofa. The lights were dim and the late-night silence surrounded them with peace.

He sipped his wine and leaned back and relaxed in the chair.

Sammie relaxed too.

"Did you enjoy your time at the ranch this weekend?" he asked.

Sammie smiled. "I did. It was great catching up with Callie. Even when we don't see each other for a long span of time, when we do it's like we'd never been apart. It's a girlfriend thing."

"Yeah, women tell me that all the time."

"I'll be seeing her a lot from now on. And when the baby comes, I'll probably make a nuisance of myself. I'll want to see him all the time."

"Yeah, you're gonna give me a run for my money as a godparent."

She chuckled and sipped wine. "I can't wait."

His voice rose to a higher pitch. "To make me look bad?"

"For the baby, silly. And you know I'm kidding. You aren't the only one around here that can tease, you know."

Jackson shook his head slightly. "I didn't know that."

"It shouldn't be a competition," Sammie said, feigning seriousness.

"But it makes life more fun when we compete." Jackson slid her a sensual look that made her nerves go raw. He lowered his voice and leaned forward, arms braced on his knees. "You want to play?"

Sammie swallowed hard and stymied the rush of lust consuming her. "Sure. I'm not afraid of going up against you."

He raised his brows and his gaze flowed over her like warm honey. "That's one way to put it."

She set her wineglass down on the cocktail table. No more alcohol for her tonight. Jackson was tempting enough without the wine to loosen her inhibitions. "I'm a little tired, Jackson."

"My cue to leave," he said, emptying his glass and rising from the chair. "It has been a long night."

She walked him to the door. "Thank you for making me feel better about the fire. I know you were upset, too. You've been really supportive and—"

"Sammie," he said, turning at the threshold and cutting her off. He wound an arm around her waist and drew her up close. He gently spread his hand under her jaw and tilted her head up.

As he brushed his lips to hers, the exquisite sensation raced to the pit of her belly. The kiss was a surprise that made her heartbeats flutter wildly. The warmth of his delicious mouth was like velvet, and after the initial shock wore off, Sammie fell further into the kiss.

He slid his hand over her throat and caressed her collarbone. Her skin prickled from the soft touch. As his lips meshed with hers, his fingers roved lower to the valley between her breasts. He grazed over the skin there and then over the tips of her breasts, making her nipples pucker. Her eyes opened wide. His touch was exquisite and exciting as he palmed over her breast in the stark darkness of her apartment doorway. Her body rang out in need. She wanted his hands all over her. She wanted his body covering her. She wanted to finally know what it was like having Jackson Worth inside her. A tiny moan escaped her lips and she surprised herself as she broke off the kiss. "We c-can't d-do this," she whispered. "We m-made a deal."

Jackson stopped short and looked at her with a pained expression. He blinked and nodded and then leaned down to join their foreheads together. His breath whispered over her cheeks. "I know. Believe it or not," he said with a deep rasp, "I'd only meant to give you a kiss good-night."

"You did," she said softly. "And then some." The effect of Jackson's kiss had her trembling still. He'd taken command of her body and now she wondered how she'd managed to work up the willpower to stop him.

"Wish I could guarantee it won't happen again."

"Jackson."

"I'm being honest, Sammie. You didn't seem to mind and don't say it was the wine."

"It wasn't the wine."

"Okay." He heaved a deep sigh and gave her a no-nonsense look. "I'm glad you had the sense to stop me. Because in another minute I was going to pick you up and haul you into your bedroom."

Sammie gulped. Sexy images came to mind of Jackson in her bed making love to her. She'd seen him naked, and it wasn't anything to sneeze at. "Can you be a little less honest?"

"Look," he said, moving away from her. "We're going to forget about me ever kissing you tonight. I'd like to think I can hold up my end of a deal."

Of course, the elephant in the room was that he'd already made love to her. But neither one of them would benefit from that reminder.

Her body still purred from the taste of heaven he'd given her tonight, but Sammie summoned up her rational side. "I can do that. I'll forget about the kiss."

"Okay, darlin'. We got us another deal."

"Yes, we do." Sammie stared at his mouth. She was sure he had other tricks in his arsenal for pleasuring a woman, but thinking like that would get her in nothing but trouble. "See you tomorrow. And Jackson?"

"What?"

"At least the kiss made me forget all about the fire."

"Glad to oblige, darlin'," he said without his usual carefree charm. He glimpsed her lips once again, then peered down at her boots and gave a slight shake of his head before walking off.

Five

Jackson slammed the door to his car and walked through the parking garage toward the elevator that would take him up to his office. This morning he'd talked with the construction foreman at Boot Barrage in detail about making the repairs and then he'd spoken with his insurance agent to make sure they'd cover the losses. Then at noon he couldn't escape a boring lunch meeting with a local politician fast enough. As he returned to his office, he briefly contemplated the mile-long list of things he wanted to accomplish, yet all through the day his thoughts had kept coming back to one thing—the good-night kiss that almost landed him in Sammie Gold's bed.

He wanted to purge last night from his memory and move on. To forget the kiss and remember that seducing her was off-limits. Period. End of story. Though Sammie could hold her own, he wouldn't take advantage of her vulnerable situation. She needed a solid business partner now, not a lover.

After one disastrous high school love affair, Jackson had vowed to never be stupid with women again and he'd already broken that rule with Sammie once. Yeah, the boots turned him on. He'd already come to terms with that, but it was his own character flaw that he feared the most. Jackson liked a challenge and he liked to win and he feared that because Sammie was forbidden fruit to him, the one girl in Arizona he couldn't go after, it made her all the more appealing to him—enough to jeopardize his relationship with his sister-in-law and brother.

He knew one thing for damn sure—he wouldn't hurt Sammie.

And live to tell about it.

Callie and Tagg would skin him alive and then toss his bones in the lake.

Jackson couldn't even crack a smile at the foolish notion.

He rode the elevator deep in thought and opened the door to his office reception room. He was immediately greeted by his secretary. "Afternoon, Mr. Worth," Betty Lou said from her desk. "How was your lunch?"

He shrugged. "Lunch with a town councilman isn't all it's cracked up to be. He's running for re-election so he gave me the full court press for a big donation."

"Are you going to back him?"

"Not sure yet. I have to give it some thought."

She nodded and handed him three messages written on note paper. "Here you go. These calls came in while you were at lunch. And," she said, clearing her throat and glancing at his closed office door, "there's someone waiting in your office."

Jackson stared at Betty Lou, waiting for more.

His secretary continued, "She didn't want to make an appointment. She insisted that you'd want to see her. And well, Jackson, I recognized her, so I figured you'd rather deal with her in your office."

Betty Lou was the mother of his childhood friend, Keith Elroy, from Red Ridge. She knew about the goings-on in town, even though she lived in the Phoenix area now. Jackson trusted her instincts and admired her loyalty. *"Her?"*

"It's me, Jackson."

Jackson turned at the lilting sound of the woman's voice. It penetrated him and brought with it old memories. Some cherished. Some painful. She stood against the doorway, her back arched, confident and smiling. Jackson's day had gone from bad to worse. "Blair."

Her lips puckered in disappointment. "I thought you'd give me a better welcome than that."

She wore red from head to toe. The shoes were thick, platform-heeled, the dress clinging to every ever-loving curve the woman had. She exposed just enough cleavage to tease a man and make him want to touch. Her face was picture-perfect with creamy porcelain skin, ruby-red-lipstick lips, clear blue eyes and long honey-wheat hair. He remembered weaving his hands through those silky strands and kissing her until he ached.

A tremor ran through his body. She was more beautiful than he remembered. "I guess you thought wrong."

She was unfazed by his comment. "I'd like to talk to you."

"I'm busy."

"I can wait right here until you're not busy." She smiled and moved her body in a way that would give any man palpitations.

He took a sharp breath and then glanced at Betty Lou. "Hold my calls."

His secretary peered at Blair Caulfield, who had a look of triumph on her face. "Will do. But you have that important meeting in thirty minutes."

Jackson gave Betty Lou a nod. The meeting was their secret way to get troublesome clients out of the office. Apparently, Betty Lou wasn't too keen on having Blair around. Unfortunately, she and all of Red Ridge knew about his heartache with Blair Caulfield. "Right. This won't take long."

He ushered Blair into his office and closed the door on Betty Lou's worried expression. He offered Blair a seat at the opposite side of his desk.

He turned away from her and strode to the window. He needed a minute. His office on the top floor of the building looked down on the busy city, with the desert and crimson mountains visible in the distance. He focused his attention there for a few moments and let the surroundings fill him with much-needed patience.

"What do you want, Blair?"

"Spoken like a man who hasn't yet forgiven me."

Jackson's jaw tightened and he turned to her. "Is that why you're here? After what, fourteen years? To ask for my forgiveness?"

She crossed one leg over the other and the material of her dress hiked up her legs. "Something like that."

Jackson didn't want to give her the satisfaction of knowing what her betrayal had cost him. The heartache had scarred him enough not to allow any woman to reopen the blistering wounds. "Okay, I forgive you. Now, if that's all you want, I'm very busy today."

She rose quickly from her seat. "You haven't forgiven me. You're still angry."

"Angry?" Jackson laughed. It hardly described the way he felt about Blair. "Because you screwed my *father's* business associate and ran away with him on the same night we were supposed to graduate from Red Ridge High School? You got him so flustered the man lost sight of his age, his honor and his dignity. Can't see why I'd still be angry about that, Blair. So give it a rest. Does your husband know you're here, asking me for forgiveness?"

Blair had allowed Jackson to take her innocence, giving him her body and what he believed to be her love. He'd fallen hard for her and made plans for their future. They'd promised to love each other until the day they died. But that hadn't been enough for the girl from the wrong side of the tracks. She'd been raised in poverty by two self-serving, self-indulgent parents who didn't care two bits about their daughter. Jackson had wanted to erase the hurt and give her everything she'd ever dreamed of. He'd been a Worth, after all. He'd come from wealth borne from hard work and he'd wanted Blair in his life forever. But he found out the night of their graduation that that hadn't been enough for stunning, impoverished Blair Caulfield. She'd hated Red Ridge. She wanted to move away from everything Jackson held dear. She'd wanted to live the high life and travel the world.

It was the one thing Jackson couldn't give her.

"My husband?" she said in a tone that suggested it was ludicrous to consider such a thing. "He's miles away from here." She lowered her lashes and admitted. "We're not together anymore."

Big surprise. Jackson had heard enough about Blair's marital history to know that she'd been on husband number three. That made her shelf life with marriage less than four years apiece. At least Jackson knew enough not to get married. He wasn't cut out for it. Blair hadn't had that same revelation yet.

He almost felt sorry for the poor suckers who'd married her.

Jackson fell silent. The ball was in her court. But Blair didn't let anything get in her way when she wanted something. "You look good, Jackson."

He stared into her beautiful eyes and said nothing.

She stepped closer to him. The scent of her expensive perfume was testimony to how much she'd changed over the years. She was a different person than the girl he'd fallen in love with in high school. "You've got nothing to say to me?"

He lifted the corner of his mouth. "You're catching on."

"I'm sorry, Jackson. I know I hurt you very much."

"It's over and done with now."

She glanced at his left hand and raised her brows. "You've never married."

"Not my style."

"It was once," she said softly, and for a second Jackson thought he heard remorse in her voice.

"What do you really want, Blair? Why'd you come to see me?"

She lifted her head and her eyes blazed with warmth. "You, Jackson. I want you back."

Jackson narrowed his eyes, secretly stunned at her admission and wondering what her angle was. She held the land he wanted in the palm of her hand, yet she hadn't mentioned it. And Jackson couldn't afford to reveal how badly he wanted that strip of land.

"Have dinner with me," she said. "Let me apologize to you properly."

He hated admitting how much seeing her again, being in the same room with her, hurt. "It's not necessary, Blair."

"Okay. Then have dinner with me for old times' sake."

"I can't tonight. I'll let you know," he said, as he strode toward the door and waited for her to leave.

Blair walked over to him with the confident air of a desirable woman. She pressed a piece of paper with her phone number written on it into his hand. "I'm staying with my aunt. Call me. Anytime."

She did everything with flair, and walking out of his office was no exception. She held her head high, her blond hair flowing over her shoulders as she caused every head at Worth Enterprises, male and female alike, to turn when she left.

Jackson cursed under his breath, quickly closed the door to his office and picked up his cell phone, punching in Sammie's number. He wasn't going to question his actions. He was running on pure instincts now and he damn well hoped they wouldn't fail him.

"I don't get it, Jackson. Why did you need to see me tonight?" Sammie thought she'd gotten a reprieve from Jackson and the memory of the good-night kiss that had caused her to lose sleep last night. But he'd called late this afternoon and insisted they have dinner together.

"I told you. We need to discuss how the repairs are going and talk about the grand opening," he said, skewering sweet and sour pork with his chopsticks.

Sammie sat across from him in his office, his spacious desk littered with Chinese take-out cartons. She savored the pungent taste of spicy Kung Pao chicken and fried rice. Arizona wasn't known for Asian cuisine, but Jackson had had the best Chinese restaurant in town deliver the food, and Sammie was enjoying every bite of her meal.

"I don't think you invited me here to talk business," Sammie said.

So far, in the forty-five minutes she'd been here, they'd talked about everything *but* business, including baseball and football. Red Sox versus Diamondbacks. Patriots versus Cardinals. Sammie knew something of sports and argued for the sake of bragging rights with him about East coast teams. He hadn't once mentioned the repairs or Boot Barrage's opening to her. She sent another delicious bit of chicken to her mouth, chewed and swallowed and then said, "I think you just wanted Chinese. And you didn't want to eat alone."

Jackson pointed his chopsticks at her. "You have a suspicious mind, Sammie."

She closed her eyes briefly. "If only that were true."

Jackson set his chopsticks down and leaned back in his I'm-the-boss leather chair. "You're talking about that jerk that left you high and dry."

She stopped eating to give him a nod. "I was gullible and naive."

"You had no reason *not* to trust him. That guy ruined your faith, and who could blame you for that? You're human, Sammie."

Sammie stared into the carton of chicken in front of her. "I didn't see it coming and I got burned."

"That makes two of us."

Sammie snapped her head up to look him square in the eyes. He'd been burned pretty badly too from what she'd been told. "Two of us?"

Jackson caught himself and his expression immediately soured. "Let's just say I know the feeling and leave it at that. Want a fortune cookie?"

He didn't wait for her to answer. The cellophane-wrapped cookie flew in her direction. She was quick in catching it. She gave him a narrow-eyed gaze, wondering about his mood tonight. Breaking open the cookie, she pulled the thin strip of paper out and read her fortune printed in red lettering. "You've got to be kidding!"

"What does it say?" Jackson asked.

"This is rigged. You had someone slip this inside the cookie, right?"

"Are you serious? You were with me when we picked up the food." He leaned forward, his gaze brimming with interest. "What in heck does it say?"

Sammie furrowed her brows. "It says, 'Good fortune is on your side. Play it for all it's *worth*.'"

Jackson busted out laughing. "No way."

His laughter made her grin, too. "I'm not joking. Here, read it yourself." She slid the fortune across the desk to him and he read it silently, smiling. "Now it's your turn."

Jackson pulled out his fortune and read it aloud. "Your good looks only exceed your great intelligence." He sent her a charming smile that made her nerves stand on end. He tossed the fortune down on top of his desk.

"It doesn't say that," she said.

"Sure does, darlin'."

"I don't believe you. Let me see it." She made a lunge for the fortune, but Jackson was too quick. He grabbed it and closed his palm so tight she heard the sound of paper crinkling in his hand.

He was pulling her leg. And she wasn't going to let him get away with it. She had a playful side too and could joke with the best of them. "You wouldn't be so hell-bent on destroying your fortune if you were telling the truth. I'm willing to bet you it doesn't say that at all."

"Now what kind of bet do you have in mind?" he asked, his eyes keen with interest.

"The kind where I win and you lose."

"Whoa. I didn't know you had a competitive side, Sammie. I'm impressed."

"What are we betting?" she asked, ready to prove him wrong.

"If you win, I'll cook you dinner."

"That's not a win," she said, shaking her head. "You don't know how to cook."

"True, but I'd hate every second of having to learn."

This was getting interesting. Sammie liked the idea of Jackson working over a hot stove. Though she cautioned herself to drop the bet and not tempt fate, her competitive nature took hold. "Okay, so if you win, which I know for a fact that you won't, then I'll cook you dinner. Anything you want."

"Anything...hmm. Okay, it's a deal."

He reached over the desk to shake her hand. Then he broke out in a wide grin. He pushed the fortune over to her. Eagerly, she picked up the tiny paper but her face fell as she read the words. "Your good looks only exceed your great intelligence," she began with a sense of dread. But as she continued to read, a gleeful sense of triumph emerged when she finished the entire sentiment, *"and yet to be humble is a greater virtue to embrace."* She leaned way back in her chair, feigning sympathy. "Oh, sorry, Jackson. You lose."

"How do you figure that?" Jackson frowned. "We bet that the fortune didn't say that I was good looking and intelligent and clearly, darlin', it did."

Sammie's eyes crossed at that logic. "That's not what the fortune said at all, Jackson. And you know it. The meaning is altogether different. You left off the most important part."

"You're splitting hairs."

"You can't possibly think you won."

He nodded. "Fair and square."

"Nope. I'm not conceding." She folded her arms across her middle and the gesture seemed to amuse him. "What?"

"You're a sore loser."

"Am not. You didn't win. I'm not cooking you dinner." Which was a relief. Sammie's culinary talents weren't all that impressive. And inviting Jackson to her apartment for a cozy home-cooked meal wouldn't be the smartest move.

"I'm sure as hell not cooking you dinner either," he said.

"Fine with me."

"Fine."

They entered into a staring contest for a long moment.

Tension crackled as both of them angled their jaws stubbornly.

Jackson was the first to break the silence. "You want to do something tonight?"

Baffled at the change in subject, she jerked her head back. "Like what?"

He shrugged. "I don't know. See a movie, maybe."

"A movie? But I thought we were supposed to talk about the grand opening."

Jackson rose from his chair, walked around his desk and took her hand. "We'll do that afterward. There's a new action adventure flick with Bruce Willis I'd love to see."

"Oh joy," Sammie said as Jackson led her out the door.

It was not a date, Sammie kept telling herself—a movie and popcorn in a stadium theater filled with a hundred or more people. Sammie wouldn't look at it as anything but a way to ease Jackson's apparent need for action-adventure. She was his movie companion, she presumed, only because she'd been handy when the thought had struck him. One of his buddies would surely have appreciated this kind of movie more than Sammie, but she'd been convenient and, admittedly, so far it hadn't been awful.

Jackson was generous with popcorn and soda, and the good thing about action flicks was that there was never a need to break out tissues and get sentimental. She just had to keep her wits about her as she viewed gratuitous blood and guts.

After the movie, Jackson rose from his seat to give his arms a good overhead stretch. He moved with the fluid grace of a cat, smooth and sure in his own skin. Sammie noticed things like that about Jackson. It was hard not to.

People filed out of the theater in orderly succession, but

Jackson seemed to be in no rush. He turned in her direction, his tone deeply satisfied. "That was good."

"Uh-huh," she said, rising as she slung her purse over her shoulder.

He chuckled at her noncommittal answer. "You hated it."

"I did not. The story had merit."

"Merit?" He leveled her a dubious look. "You don't have to lie. Next time, we'll go see something you'd like to see. But I'm warning you in advance, I don't do sappy, unless Jennifer Aniston is in it." He grinned.

Next time? Sammie wanted to shake out her ears. Pretending not to hear his comment, she fiddled with her purse straps.

"Ready for ice cream?" he asked as he moved along the already empty aisle.

"Oh—uh." She couldn't think fast enough to come up with an excuse to say no. "What time is it?"

Jackson glanced at his watch. "It's a quarter till it's-always-a-good-time-for-ice-cream."

Sammie couldn't help her smile as she warned herself again that this wasn't a date. Jackson must have had a rough day because he seemed to want to indulge in his favorite things tonight. "I bet you know where the best ice-cream place in town is."

He only smiled and led her outside the theater toward his truck.

Half an hour later, they sat in Sonny Side Up eating six different flavors of ice cream.

"I think I like Cherry Chip Jubilee the best," she said after sliding the spoon out of her mouth.

"Five Times Fudge has my vote," Jackson said, finishing up his dish and leaning back in the café's seat.

Sammie tilted her head, relishing the taste of sweet cherries, walnuts and creamy vanilla ice cream. "You're sure

Sonny doesn't mind us barging into his place in the middle of the night like this?"

"He won't mind."

"What'd he do, lose a bet or something?"

Jackson laughed. "You're astute."

"Flies don't land on me," Sammie said, repeating a common phrase she'd heard at Worth Ranch recently.

"Apparently not, darlin'." Jackson dangled the keys in front of her. They were on a sterling silver key chain with the initials JLW etched into a leather strap. "It was a basketball bet. That guy loses so dang often, he finally just gave me the key to his place."

"It's a nice setup. Every time you beat him up on the court, you get free ice cream."

Jackson nodded with a twinkle in his eyes. "But I rarely take him up on it."

That surprised her. He'd walked into the place as though he'd done it a hundred times before. "Why not?"

"I don't know. It's more about winning than indulging." He shrugged. "I've got to be in the mood for ice cream."

Or in *a* mood. Sammie was sensing that Jackson needed a friend tonight. And silly her, she thought that perhaps she'd just glided into that position.

"So what happens if you lose?"

He rubbed the back of his neck and sighed. "You don't really want to know."

Sammie blinked and narrowed her eyes. "I sure as heck want to know."

It was an innocent question that Jackson seemed reluctant to answer.

"I could lie."

"I would know."

He sighed again, quietly. "You probably would know," he said, as if that fact annoyed him. "It's nothing much really. If I lose, then Sonny gets the use of my penthouse for a night or two."

Sammie caught his drift immediately. Her cheeks flamed. "Oh. I see…and I take it, it's not for watching sports on your gigantic flat-screen television."

Though she'd never seen it, she'd bet her best pair of high-heeled silver-sequined boots that Jackson's penthouse apartment was a man cave filled with everything necessary to seduce a woman. Her imagination ran wild and she found herself dying to know more. She made a mental note to ask Callie about it. Her mouth inadvertently turned down with a wry twist.

Jackson added, "For the record, he's never taken me up on it."

"He never wins?"

"Hell has frozen over a few times."

Slowly, Sammie nodded. "Well, you don't have to worry. I won't say a word. It's a man thing, right?" There was more accusation in her tone than she intended.

Jackson shrugged. He spoke not so much in his own defense but perhaps as a veiled warning to her. "I'm a bachelor, Sammie. It goes with the territory."

He wasn't telling her something she didn't already know. She wondered how many women thought they could change Jackson's mind about bachelorhood and steer him toward marriage. She reminded herself to never fall into that category.

Sammie changed the subject and the conversation finally turned to the grand opening. For the remainder of the evening they discussed her plans. It felt good to be on solid ground again. With Jackson's assurances that Boot Barrage would open on the newly scheduled date, Sammie could focus all of her attention on making the place a success.

Later, when Jackson brought her home, he thanked her

for a nice evening and they joked about how much ice cream they'd eaten. He didn't linger at her door and Sammie was grateful. Jackson still made her heart ping, but that was only because of his irresistible good looks and charm. It wasn't that she had feelings for him.

There was nothing wrong with a woman having a good old-fashioned healthy dose of lust. She'd be in the minority if she didn't find Jackson attractive. And with that thought in mind, Sammie went to bed thinking about luscious cherry chips, deep dark fudge and caramel topping.

She would dream good dreams tonight.

Her alarm went off precisely at 6:00 a.m. Her eyes opened to thin seams of light breaking through the smooth white wooden slats in her bedroom window. It was autumn in the desert, where temperatures still rose above the national average. Her room warmed easily with sunshine streaming in. She wasn't sure she liked the lack of seasons in Arizona and thought once again about the leaves turning color in Massachusetts.

She got out of bed and ignored the tempting desire to curl back up under the covers to sleep another hour. She ate a light breakfast of oatmeal with blueberries and juice and then changed into her workout clothes—a pair of running pants and a tank top. She slid two clips into her hair to keep her bangs back and washed her face. Twenty minutes later, with a fanny pack around her waist and a pair of sunglasses on, she took to the residential streets of Scottsdale in a slow-paced run.

She'd been a runner in high school and had jogged regularly in college, but lately she'd been slack in her exercise regimen. It was her time for fresh starts and as she jogged the streets, she waved at her neighbors who were also up early, smiled at fellow joggers and nodded at dedicated dog-walkers on a leisurely stroll.

With a slight breeze ruffling her hair, her legs eating pavement and her mind free, Sammie thoroughly enjoyed her run. She was at least two miles from her apartment and cutting into a beautiful public park when she came face-to-face with Sonny Estes. It took her a second to recognize him in dark sunglasses running along the same pathway but coming from the opposite direction. He filled out a neat white T-shirt and navy sweat pants. The instant he spotted her he jogged over and fell in step beside her. Both slowed their pace so they could talk.

"So, you're a runner," he said.

"Used to be. I'm trying to get back into it," she huffed out. Back in the day, she could run for five miles before feeling slightly winded.

"You're doing great," Sonny said with a note of admiration.

Sammie wished she could believe that, but the last half mile had been a killer. "Thanks. But you had to slow to a snail's pace to match me. I haven't run seriously for years."

"Well, you fooled me."

"No kidding. I'm really dying inside. Everything is going to ache tomorrow."

Sonny chuckled. They ran past a sandy playground filled with colorful blue and orange slides, swings and jungle gyms. In a few hours the park would be alive with small smiling children, but now it was deserted and quiet. "Do you run every day?" she asked.

"Every day but Sunday. I come by this way often."

"That's good to know."

He shot her a long glance, his brows rising well above his shades before giving her an interested smile. "Are you up for a regular running companion?"

Sammie directed her attention forward. She hadn't been flirting, but Sonny might have taken it that way. "I'd never keep up with you, but thanks anyway."

"I bet you could," he said with an acknowledging nod, but thankfully he didn't press the issue. There was no way Sammie could keep the vigorous pace that she'd seen when he'd first approached her.

They ran side by side for a while. She was admittedly out of shape. Her breaths came in short bursts. Her legs burned with fatigue. She took long pulls of oxygen, struggling to keep going. She was a fighter, her father had often said with pride. Sammie tried to remember that as she pressed on and ran another mile beside Sonny. But finally she slowed and Sonny did the same. They'd rounded the park and were heading back in the direction of her apartment. "I'm about through. I can't go anymore. I'm going to walk the rest of the way home."

"I'll walk with you," he said resolutely.

"You don't have to do that. I've already ruined your run."

He laughed. "Not true. I was almost through with my run when we met. I went two miles farther than I usually do. I'm dying inside, too."

He didn't look like he was dying at all. He'd barely broken a sweat. Every dark hair on his head was still neatly in place. He was muscular and tanned and good-looking and suddenly Sammie thought, why not? He was nice enough and she could use a friend. "Okay. We'll walk back to my place and I'll give you a cold drink. Unless you have to open Sonny Side Up up?"

Sonny grinned at her little joke and shook his head. "My younger brother, Bobby, opens the place for me in the mornings."

They walked the rest of the way back making small talk and getting to know one another. It was nearly eight o'clock when they arrived at her apartment for a glass of cold water. Ten minutes later, after showing him her small apartment, she walked Sonny to her front door.

"Remember, I owe you lunch at my place," he said.

"Oh, about that. I was already there. Last night." She'd felt a little guilty about not mentioning it to him earlier, but there never seemed to be a right time. "Jackson and I had ice cream. Apparently, you lost a bet."

Good-naturedly, he replied, "Ah, so you're the one."

She blinked. "You know about it?"

"I got a text from Jackson that he was there last night. He didn't say he brought a date, but I figured as much."

"I wasn't his date." Sammie's voice rose sharply and Sonny gave her an odd look. She went on to explain, "We went to a movie and then he wanted to stop for ice cream."

"So, you're not dating Jackson?"

"No, of course not. We're in business together and I'm a close family friend. That's about all." She cringed at how adamant her denial sounded. Sammie couldn't imagine actually dating Jackson Worth. Once he turned on the full force of his charm, with his drop-dead good looks and Western swagger, he'd make it hard for any woman to see straight, much less keep their wits about them. Jackson had been careful around her even though they'd had a whopper of a misstep in Las Vegas. That was over and done with. Sammie was glad that they had developed a solid working relationship over the past few weeks and that both had one goal in mind—to launch Boot Barrage with great fanfare and style. "I'm not dating anyone at the moment."

Heavens, how could she be? She'd only been in Arizona a short time. Some women attracted men like bees to honey, but that had never been the case with her. She wasn't a femme fatale. The only sense of flair and style about her involved the boots she wore.

Sonny's eyes lit with a gleam. "That's very good to know, Sammie."

His disarming smile made her realize he was flirting.

"I enjoyed our run," he said. "Maybe we'll *run* into each other again sometime."

Sammie smiled and decided she didn't mind Sonny Estes flirting with her. "Maybe we will."

As a matter of fact, Sammie had enjoyed the run, too. She'd pressed herself to go farther with Sonny at her side and one thing could be said about vigorous exercise…it might kill you while you're doing it, but you're never sorry afterward that you'd pushed yourself hard. She'd have to reconsider having a running partner once Boot Barrage was operating smoothly. But for now, she had enough on her plate.

After Sonny left, she headed straight for the shower. She had interviews to conduct later this morning. She hoped to find part-time help for Boot Barrage by the end of the week.

The shower was steamy and invigorating. She luxuriated in it for a few extra minutes, letting the easy rain of water soothe the knots in her muscles. Once they loosened up, her whole body relaxed. She'd been wound tight lately and she attributed the tension to all the changes in her life.

She stepped out of the shower and dried off using a plush white cotton towel, then towel-dried her hair, laughing at herself as she took a look in the mirror. Her short locks were standing on end in crazy, pointy spikes, Lady Gaga style. "Sammie, you're a rock star."

Maybe the college kids from Arizona State University would be more inclined to interview for her if she looked like this. She set that silly notion aside and took her time dressing in leg-hugging slacks and a white tailored blouse under a sleeveless pewter-colored vest. She picked out a pair of boots cuffed in suede with tall platform heels. Her attire today would say "hip" yet professional.

A knock at the door sounded, startling Sammie. She wasn't expecting anyone at nine in the morning. She went to the door and peeked through the peephole.

Her breath caught—she hated the reaction she had every time Jackson Worth appeared in her line of vision. "Sammie, it's me. Open up."

Six

"What do you mean, you postponed my interviews today?" Sammie got over her bout of man-lust as soon as Jackson had walked inside her apartment and announced he'd told Betty Lou to reschedule the appointments she had lined up. Since Boot Barrage was still under construction, Sammie had set up the interviews for this morning at the Worth offices.

"First off, they were *our* interviews," Jackson said casually.

"Technically, that's not true," Sammie argued. She was a little peeved that he'd taken the liberty to postpone the interviews without discussing it with her first. He was a hands-on kind of business partner, but Sammie wanted to do this part mostly by herself. It was the one thing she could contribute to the partnership without feeling like a big, fat charity case. "You were going to have final approval once

I picked the candidates for the job. At least that's what you told me. Why'd you cancel?"

His gaze lifted to her hair and she shuddered. She'd forgotten about the wild spikes and total lack of makeup on her face. "Is that a new look?"

Damn him for showing up unannounced. But she wouldn't give him the satisfaction of seeing her squirm. "What if it is?"

He glanced at her whole outfit, down to her Italian-made silver-gray suede boots. He studied them for a second before answering. "I'd say, go for it."

"No, you wouldn't."

Jackson grinned. "It's different."

"Wait here," she ordered.

Admittedly mortified, Sammie strode to the bathroom and picked up her hair brush. As she turned toward the mirror with brush in hand, she rolled her eyes when Jackson appeared. Their eyes met through the mirror's reflection. "What part of 'wait here' don't you understand?"

Jackson leaned against the bathroom doorjamb with arms folded and let out a belly laugh that echoed in the tiny bathroom.

She couldn't blame Jackson for his amusement. Her hair stood on end as if she'd put her finger in an electrical socket. She took another glimpse at him and then looked back at her reflection before she giggled. "Okay, I do look ridiculous. Give me a minute to fix this. And while I'm combing out my hair, you might want to tell me why on earth you postponed those appointments."

"Tagg and I have been called out of town for the day. We're flying to Tucson."

Sammie tugged especially hard on a lock of her hair as she caught sight of him in her mirror again. So, it was back to that. "I am perfectly capable of interviewing part-time help without you, Jackson."

He nodded. "I don't doubt you, Sammie. That's not the reason I postponed the interviews. Tagg called early this morning. He's worried about leaving Callie. She's been hormonal, as you ladies say, and he doesn't want her up at Red Ridge all alone today. He needs a favor from you. Will you stay with Callie while we're gone?"

Stunned by the request and glad to help Callie for any reason, she leveled him a puzzled look. "Well, why didn't you say so in the first place?"

He grinned. "I was distracted."

By her hair. She frowned. "Of course I'll go. Callie is due in two weeks. I don't want her to be alone either. Why didn't you call?"

"I did call. You didn't answer your phone this morning."

"Oh, right. I was out." And she hadn't bothered to check her voice mail messages. No one usually called her before eight in the morning.

His brows furrowed. "Out? So early?"

She nodded with a shrug of her shoulders. Jackson stared at her for a long drawn-out moment, waiting for an explanation, and Sammie decided right then not to elaborate. He didn't need to know everything about her. A girl had to have a few secrets.

When he finally figured out she wasn't going to say more, Jackson said, "So I was right to postpone the interviews. Being as I couldn't reach you, I figured you'd want to spend time with Callie and all."

Sammie concentrated extra hard on her comb out, refusing to look at him again and ignoring his comment.

"I thought so," he added breezily.

She could only imagine the width of his smug grin.

It was strange having Jackson watching her. How exciting was it for a man to watch a woman spray her hair, curl mascara onto her eyelashes and pick out the right color of lipstick to match her clothes? But she'd asked him once already to wait in the living room and that request had gone by the wayside. There wasn't time to argue with him, so she endured the few minutes of his scrutiny and told herself it didn't matter. What was important today was getting to Red Ridge to be with her friend. "Did Tagg say if Callie was upset about anything in particular?"

She met his gaze again in the mirror as she leaned close to pucker her lips. With a twist, she unwound the wand of lipstick and angled the tip to her mouth. Jackson watched with keen interest while she slashed lipstick across her lips, smacked them together for even distribution and then blotted her mouth with a tissue.

"He, uh…he said she'd cry up a storm if he looked at her sideways."

She turned to face him, noting his focus on her light-rose-colored lips. A tremor passed through her but she locked her mind on to Callie and not the way Jackson was looking at her. "He's exaggerating, I hope."

Jackson shook his head. "No. Tagg wasn't complaining about her. It was more like he didn't know how to help her."

Sammie let that sink in and worked faster at finishing her grooming. Poor Callie. She carried a watermelon-sized little baby inside her belly—it was only natural that she'd have bouts of emotion as rocky as the Red Ridge Mountains.

When Sammie finally finished with her makeup, she turned around and was struck by the startling impact of Jackson's approving gaze. His eyes lit on every aspect of her, from her newly transformed hairdo to her slightly made-up face to her semi-professional clothes and lastly to her pewter cuffed suede boots. A low rumble of appreciation slipped easily from his lips. "Very nice."

And just as easily a thrill of satisfaction wrapped itself around her. A compliment from a charmer shouldn't be taken too seriously, but Jackson looked truly sincere. She liked him better when he was giving her grief so she could give it back to him and tell herself he was way out of her league. But when he looked at her as if she could win a beauty pageant… No, she wasn't going there. "I take it you want to drive together."

He nodded lazily. "Makes sense with gas prices such as they are."

"Tagg doesn't want to inconvenience me." Sammie was thinking out loud. The Worths had enough money combined to buy a dozen prolific oil fields. The price of gas was not the issue here.

"It's hard for him to ask anyone for a favor, darlin'. He wants to make it easy for you."

Being with Jackson wasn't easier for her than driving alone up to Red Ridge, but now wasn't the time for that discussion. "He's a considerate man. What time is your meeting in Tucson?"

"One o'clock. We'll be having a late lunch and hope to be back at the ranch by six. I know Tagg will be itching to get home. If it wasn't so dang important that he show up, I'd go by myself. But Tagg's the numbers man and the meeting is very important to Worth Enterprises. If it gets too late for you, we can stay over at the ranch tonight."

Oh, no "we" couldn't. She shook her head. "I can't. I have an appointment with a local vendor early in the morning. But if that's a problem, I'll be happy to drive myself."

Jackson straightened, unfolded his arms and spoke with determination. "Not a problem at all. We'll drive back together."

Inside, Sammie gave herself a mental shake. All this "we" stuff simply had to get easier to digest. She and Jackson

weren't a pair in any way that mattered. She hoped that after
Boot Barrage launched Jackson would turn his attention
elsewhere, but her hope for that happening sort of fizzled as
soon as she remembered about Rory's upcoming birth and
all of the times she and Jackson would be thrust together
for Worth family events.

Sammie gave Jackson a halfhearted smile and then gathered up her things. "I'm ready."

Jackson laid a hand on the small of her back and guided
her outside. Having his fingers splaying gently across her
spine was like lighting a flame to a torch.

Sammie sighed, resigning herself to her lot in life—to be
forever turned on by the most out of reach man on the planet.

Once they got out of town, the drive to Red Ridge went
relatively quickly. The open roads allowed a legally higher
speed limit than anywhere she could remember. There were
no crowds on the highways, no gridlock parking lots like
in Boston, where movement went from five miles an hour
to barely noticeable. Jackson spent most of his time on his
speaker phone with business associates and his secretary,
while Sammie decided to enjoy the scenery as they approached Worth Ranch.

The solid earth and surrounding mountains laid claim to
gorgeous midmorning sunlit hues of crimson and copper.
Only the sky was blue, daring to contrast with Arizona's
natural color palette.

Sammie drank in the view, and as they drove onto Worth
property, the scent of grazing cattle and rawhide reached
her nostrils. It was also the scent of great wealth, of perse-
verance, of loyalty and great family history. Sammie envied
Jackson that. He'd always known who he was and where he
belonged. He had deep family roots, something Sammie had
only dreamed about.

Growing up, Sammie thought she was on her way to all the good things that life had in store for her. Nothing had turned out as she'd hoped. But she wouldn't dwell on the past. She had already put her horrible experience with Allen from her mind, yet the lessons she'd learned would stay with her for a lifetime. She would never trust again, not in the way she had before, and that thought saddened her. She'd been robbed of more than money, and that loss she felt way down deep in her soul.

"Have you come up with a game plan for Callie yet? You've already shopped your eyeballs out."

She chuckled and shook her head at Jackson's nonsense. He had it all and maybe he knew it, but she couldn't fault him for being who he was. He'd been more than decent to her. Why couldn't he be a jerk and give her cause to dislike him?

"Sometimes doing nothing at all will cure what ails you. We'll just hang out and talk."

Jackson gave her a piercing look, his gaze filled with silent warning.

"Don't worry. You won't be the topic of conversation."

"I'm not worried, darlin'. We've got us a little secret. And I trust you to keep it."

There was that "we" again. Sammie winced inwardly. When would it end?

Sammie had been tempted many a time to tell Callie the truth. She hated keeping a secret this big from her best friend. But good sense had prevailed over the guilt she felt. Today would be all about making Callie feel better. And if she couldn't do that, then Sammie would find a way to distract her.

When Jackson parked in front of Tagg and Callie's house on the hill, Callie came out to greet them with Tagg lumbering behind wearing a worried expression. He carried a black leather briefcase in one hand. He looked about as eager to leave his wife as a man going to his own execution.

Jackson bounded out of the truck and came around to open Sammie's door. The gesture didn't go unnoticed. Jackson had good manners. Once she got out, she thanked him and turned her attention to her friend.

Callie rushed into her arms and they hugged tight. Then Callie quietly scolded her. "I love that you came for a visit, Sammie. But I know why you're here and you didn't have to take time from your busy schedule to come all this way to babysit me. I'm fine."

She wasn't fine. Callie had red splotches around her eyes and she looked pale. She'd been crying, and Sammie believed Tagg's claim of utter frustration in not being able to help her. Sometimes men didn't get it. Only another woman could sympathize with tricky, uninvited, devilish hormones. "I really didn't come to babysit you," she said, thinking on her feet. Somehow her idea of claiming to want to hang out together wouldn't cut it. "I actually need *your* help with something. If you have the time later, I could use some advice."

"Really?" Callie asked, her ashen face lighting up.

"Uh-huh. Really."

From behind, Tagg sent Sammie a look of gratitude, his eyes filling with relief right before he gave her a big hug.

"We've got to get going," Jackson said, glancing at his watch.

Tagg heaved a big sigh. "Okay. Yeah, we should get on the road."

Then he turned to Callie. He gave her the sweetest look in the world, one that women of all ages would understand, and took her into his arms with so much care it nearly brought tears to Sammie's eyes.

"I love you," Tagg said from somewhere deep in his throat.

"I love you, too," Callie said.

And then Tagg kissed her. It was so intimate, so unbelievably tender that Sammie had to look away for fear of invading their privacy. Unfortunately, she turned toward Jackson, who was watching her with sharp assessing eyes. Their gazes locked and lingered. She hoped to hide the dire longing from her expression, but Sammie wasn't really all that great with concealing her emotions.

The mood was instantly broken when Jackson gave her a playful wink before turning away.

Sammie returned her gaze to her friends, suddenly envious of everyone who had ever been truly in love. Not that she'd begrudge Callie and Tagg their happiness—they were perfect for each other and, heaven knew, their road to matrimony hadn't been easy. But Sammie was beginning to wonder if she'd ever look at someone the way Callie looked at Tagg. Or if a man would ever treasure her in the same way Tagg cherished his wife.

Just as those thoughts were beginning to depress her, Tagg did a remarkable thing. The rugged cowboy bent his head and with genuine tenderness kissed the roundest part of Callie's belly. As he whispered fatherly words to his unborn son, Sammie caught the tail end of what he was saying. "Be a good boy and stay put in there until Daddy returns. Remember, I love you, too."

Callie touched her hand to Tagg's head, weaving fingers through his dark hair and in that moment Sammie's eyes did well up. A painful burn invaded her belly and deep yearning threatened to destroy her friend's sweetest moment, so Sammie managed, and not without struggle, to hold back her tears.

"He'll wait," Callie assured him.

"I'm only a quick plane ride away, so just call if you need me," Tagg said, his eyes soft on his wife.

Their gazes lingered until finally Callie gave her husband a little shove. "Go. I'm fine. Sammie will be here."

With that, the men bid them farewell and got into the car. Sammie stood in front of the house with Callie until Tagg and Jackson had driven down the road and out of sight.

In that instant, Sammie knew *how* she wanted to be loved. If that day ever came, it would be all or nothing for her. She wanted the same kind of bond Tagg and Callie had, to cherish the one she loved and have him feel exactly the same way about her. She wanted to know what it was like to give someone her full trust again with her whole heart.

Nothing else would do.

On a sigh, she wound her arm around Callie's shoulder and they walked side by side into the house.

An hour later, Sammie tossed a roast beef salad with hard-boiled eggs, shredded carrots, dill pickles, hearts of palm, asparagus and green olives. "Callie's Cravings Salad is ready," Sammie said as she set the wooden bowl on the table. "All your favorites and there's enough for leftovers."

Callie glanced at the half-gallon-sized bowl. "What, no chocolate chips?"

Sammie chuckled. She was glad she'd come today. Already Callie's mood seemed lighter. "Next time, my friend."

"I can't believe you're going to eat this with me."

Sammie set two dishes onto the sage-green straw placemats on the kitchen table. "Why not? It's my own creation and I like all this stuff, too."

Callie brought over a pitcher of lemonade. "But all of this together is pretty gruesome for someone not craving it. I shouldn't make you eat this."

Sammie gestured for her to sit down and then she took a seat. "It's okay, dig in."

The salad wasn't awful, and if it helped Callie feel better, Sammie didn't mind eating it.

A few minutes into the meal, Callie asked, "Do you really need my advice about something important?"

"I wouldn't say that it's life-threatening or anything. But I, uh…do have something to ask you. Have you met Sonny Estes? You know, the guy who owns Sonny Side Up?"

"Once or twice. He seems like a good guy. Jackson's his landlord, I think."

Sammie nodded. "That's right. His place is down the street from Boot Barrage."

She was curious about Sonny, and she'd been giving his invitation to be his running partner some thought. "I literally ran into him this morning. I was jogging and so was he. We took a run together."

"So what's up?" Callie asked point-blank, setting her fork down.

She shrugged. "I don't know. He was sort of flirting with me, I think. But maybe not. I've been burned so badly, I'm not even sure if I'm reading signals right anymore. This morning he asked me if I wanted a running partner."

"And you're afraid to even think about starting something up with someone, right?"

Sammie sighed. She really wondered if she knew how to deal with the opposite sex anymore. But at least it felt good to get this off her chest. "I think he wants to ask me out. I don't know if I'm ready."

Callie touched Sammie's arm gently. "I think you'll know when you're ready. It's natural to be gun-shy after what you've gone through."

"And I'm going to be so busy." She was making excuses.

"But a running partner isn't exactly an invitation to marriage, Sam. You could take him up on it and see where it leads. If you like him, maybe that's not a bad thing."

"I don't know."

Suddenly, Jackson's face flashed into her mind. Oh, who was she kidding? He'd been on her mind a lot lately, and the thought of starting a relationship with a man who wasn't Jackson Worth made her cringe. She'd spent too much time around him these past few weeks. He was the bar that no other man could ascend to and she was irritated that she felt that way. She'd be nothing but a fool to give in to feelings for Jackson.

Damn him anyway.

Callie patted her arm. "I can ask Jackson about him if you'd like. They've been friends for a while."

"Oh, no. That's not necessary. I'll work it out. I just wanted to run it by you to see what you think."

"Okay. I'm glad you did." Callie smiled and rubbed her tummy. Her skin stretched tight when the baby moved. The birth was getting close now. Soon little Rory would be here. "Whenever you have something to discuss you know where I live. You can always talk to me. About *anything*."

Oh, how she wished that were true. Guilt clocked in again, right on cue, whenever Jackson's name came up. It wasn't so much that's she'd slept with him, but that both were covering it up that made her feel like she was betraying her best friend. Honesty was a virtue that Sammie had always prided herself on.

"Speaking of Jackson, how is my brother-in-law doing today?"

"Today? Fine I guess. Why?"

"Because, I heard that the love of his life paid him a visit."

Sammie's heart squeezed tight hearing that news. "He didn't mention anything."

"No, I don't suppose he would since you're new in town. You don't know their history. But he told Tagg. It's no big secret really. Everyone at his office saw Blair Caulfield there yesterday afternoon so it's okay that I tell you. By now, Betty Lou's grapevine would have reached half the people in Red Ridge."

"Yesterday?" Sammie's voice squeaked, but before Callie grew suspicious of the pitch in her voice, she tempered her tone. "He saw her yesterday?"

Callie nodded.

Now it all made sense. The reason Jackson had insisted on seeing her last night. On having Chinese and taking her to a movie and then inviting her for ice cream afterward. He'd been rattled and needed a diversion. Or at least a distraction from what was probably a difficult encounter. She didn't know why she was angry about that. Or why she felt slightly used, even though Jackson hadn't tried to kiss her again. Sammie had just been a convenient tool to help him get through a bad day.

"Yes, she just showed up unannounced at his office," Callie said. "And get this…she said she wants him back. After what she's done to him. After all these years."

Sammie's heart began pounding against her ribs. "So he told her no, right?"

"According to Tagg, he didn't tell her anything one way or the other. Honestly, I'm surprised that he didn't boot her out of his office. I know he can handle his own affairs, but I worry about him sometimes."

Sammie fought the raw emotions threatening to swallow her up. Jackson didn't say no? To a woman who'd nearly destroyed him and ruined him for love. There could only be one reason why. He was considering it. He was still in love with her.

Sammie wondered why she was reacting this way. What had happened between her and Jackson was a mistake and well forgotten. She didn't want to feel the jealousy that was consuming her and making her inwardly squirm with dread.

Thankfully, Callie changed the subject. After lunch, Sammie helped Callie fold and put away all of Rory's newly laundered baby clothes. Callie's excitement over her little boy's upcoming arrival and just being in the baby's nursery helped calm Sammie down.

She shoved thoughts about Jackson Worth out of her mind.

There was too much at stake to give in to her emotions and frankly, right now she wasn't sure it was worth the risk.

Sammie sat ramrod stiff in the car as Jackson drove away from Tagg and Callie's house later that evening. He turned her way several times to comment about his day, yet she'd refused to spare him a glance. Her answers to his questions were short and to the point.

"Did you have a nice time with Callie today?"

"Yes."

"She seemed all right when we left. You must have cheered her up today."

"I suppose."

"What'd you ladies do?"

"We talked mostly."

"Right, you had some advice to ask her. Or were you making that up?"

"I wasn't making it up."

Jackson noted her clipped tone and reached over the armrest to take her hand. "Hey, what's wrong? Is something bothering you?"

His touch sent spirals of heat to her belly. How easy it was for him to touch her and not feel anything. How easy it was for him to be comfortable with her. She'd only had to take one look at him today when he'd returned with Tagg before her heartbeats sped up and her breath caught. She'd never hated her reaction to him more than right now.

Before he'd gotten into the car he'd taken off his dark suit jacket, loosened his silk tie and pulled it over his head. Now he sped down the road with two buttons unfastened on his dress shirt, the sleeves rolled onto his bronzed forearms and his hand loose and confident on the steering wheel. With the car windows down and the sunroof opened, his wheat-colored, collar-length hair tossed around. The windswept look just underscored his deadly gorgeous appearance.

Sammie glanced down at the hand covering hers. His fingers were long and groomed, but rough too against her softer skin. "No, nothing. I'm just tired."

Tired of pretending Jackson Worth wasn't the most devastating man she'd ever met.

Tired of fighting her feelings for him.

Tired of being weak when she should be strong.

He gave her hand a squeeze. "Why don't you close your eyes? Take a little rest."

It sounded like a good idea. It had been a long, eventful day and tomorrow would be just as busy.

"When you wake up we'll be home."

She ignored the "we" and took his advice. She closed her eyes.

Not five minutes later Jackson's foul language jarred her peaceful rest. "Sonofabitch!"

The car was pitching to the side. Winds howled and Jackson immediately closed the sunroof and windows.

She sat up straight and stared at him. "What is it?"

She didn't like the look on Jackson's face and when she followed the direction of his gaze and saw what held his rapt attention, her eyes went wide with astonishment. "Oh, my God."

A mile-wide wall of dust barreled toward them. Sammie had never seen anything like it. It towered into the sky, covering everything like a reddish-gray blanket that moved faster than storm clouds. But this enormous cloud seemed to come from the ground up. She'd been in hurricanes, floods and even a small tornado once in her life, but nothing compared to this giant monster approaching.

"Hang on, darlin'." He meant that literally, so she gripped the edges of her seat. "Damn, I didn't see it coming until we hit that rise. Wind's kicking up really fast."

It was an understatement. Trees lining the road bent in half fighting the high-speed gusts. And they were heading straight into it.

"Can we turn back?"

"We can't outrun it," Jackson said. "It's gonna be bad."

Fear slammed her chest and she froze, holding back panic. There wasn't anyone else on the road. "Jackson?"

"Don't be scared, Sammie. I've got an idea."

It was too late for that. She was terrified. "O-kay."

He scanned the road, which was barely visible at this point. Their surroundings went black—every road sign and tree had disappeared into the smoky dust monster. Winds battered the car as he drove off the main road. The truck trudged on. "Won't be long now, if I'm remembering correctly."

Sammie didn't ask any questions. Jackson's full concentration focused on seeing the road, which was illuminated by his headlights ten feet in front of him. All else was hidden by the windy gusts of the dust wall.

Violent tremors of fear wracked her body. She shook everywhere but managed to hang on to her seat, silently praying. She envisioned being swallowed up and spit out by the incredible beast. Her only consolation was in seeing the look of determination on Jackson's face.

"Unless I miss my guess, we're almost there. How're you doing?"

He actually expected her to speak? Her teeth were rattling

around in her head, but she managed a few words rather than have Jackson break concentration to look at her. "D-don't worry about m-me."

Shortly, he pulled the car to a stop in the middle of *nowhere*. "This should be it."

There was nothing around. Sammie wondered if Jackson had lost his marbles. She didn't see anything in front, in back or to the side of her. "Where are we?"

"Stay put, Sammie. I'm gonna check it out. Be back in a sec."

"What?"

He got out of the car, fighting the powerful gusts to shut the door. In the dim headlights, she saw him sway and shift in the wind and then he disappeared from view.

A minute later the door whipped open and Jackson was there. "Okay, grab what you need," he shouted against the noisy howls of the wind.

She gripped her purse and before she knew it, Jackson lifted her off her seat and into his arms. He used his rear end to slam the door shut. "Put your body tight against mine and duck your head," he shouted, struggling to be heard over the gusts. Then he shielded her body with his as he carried her out of the headlights and into the dark.

Seven

Jackson could see that Sammie was petrified. This wasn't the best kind of initiation to Arizona life, he thought as he carried her down the narrow staircase that led to the Stubbings' bunker. He wasn't sure what he would find down here, but it was shelter and it would be safe.

He'd handed Sammie his phone and the dim light from the screen illuminated the staircase. He'd already counted eight steps and he continued on down a few more before he reached the bottom. Sammie was clinging to him for dear life. "It's okay, darlin', don't be scared."

"I'm n-not scared," she said, pulling tighter on his neck.

Jackson stifled a smile. Sammie's first dust storm was frightening the stuffing right out of her. He hadn't seen one this huge before either. Once he'd gotten over that rise and bore witness to the size of it, he knew it was going to be a record-breaking event. The dust wall spread out like an evil cloak to seal the darkness and violence inside. Even now, after closing and tightly securing the hatch door, Jackson could hear the deafening sound of the winds that blew the dust a mile high and who knew how many miles wide.

The door to the hatch rattled but not enough to cause a threat.

"I'm going to set you down now."

Her voice was tiny in the darkened space. "Okay."

"Okay?" he asked to be sure.

Her hair tickled the underside of his chin. She smelled fresh, like peaches again, and the scent contrasted sharply with the musty odor of the bunker.

He lowered her legs first and once her feet hit solid ground he held her upright. She'd been shaking and now he wondered if her legs would hold her.

"I'll hold on to you for a while."

He held her tight, giving her warmth. She didn't protest or utter a word but stayed in his arms. He felt slight tremors grip her body. Sammie had to be unnerved to stay silent so long.

Finally, she asked in a whisper, "Where are we?"

He kept his voice low and calm. "In Benjamin Stubbing's bunker."

"How...how did you know about this place?"

"I used to play here with his sons. The old man was a survivalist. We would sneak in and hold secret meetings when we were ten years old. Later, I'd bring...uh...never mind."

"You'd bring girls here?" Sammie asked in a hushed tone.

He nodded. "But only to impress them. They thought it was neat."

"I'll bet they thought *you* were neat."

Jackson's mouth curved up. That much he couldn't deny. He had a reputation with women, but Sammie's vivid imagination far exceeded any real-life encounters he might have had with them. He took the cell phone from her hand. "We're almost out of charge, darlin'. Let me look around and see what I can find."

He scrounged around in the dark, bumping into a table and nearly knocking over something heavy that was sitting on its edge. He quickly grabbed the object before it fell onto the ground—it was a battery-charged flashlight. With the help of the light from his phone, he found the switch to turn it on. A circle of light five feet wide illuminated the bunker. "We're in luck. We have light and…" He noticed that the table wasn't a table at all but a cabinet with two good-sized doors. He opened them to find a wealth of sealed packages containing food, water and blankets. "We won't starve."

"Eating is the last thing on my mind," Sammie whispered with a shiver.

For the first time Jackson took note of how cold it was in the bunker. Sammie's shivers weren't just from fright. He grabbed one of the compacted thin emergency thermal blankets from the cabinet. "I can take care of heating us up."

"I never had a doubt."

He swung the flashlight until the ring of light fell around Sammie. She looked small and fragile standing in the middle of the room, but that didn't stop her quick wit or the way she had of making him smile. He looked past her toward the wall of the bunker. "Just as I remembered. There's a bunk bed behind you."

Sammie turned to look at it. "You think it's sturdy?"

"If you knew Ben, you'd know that answer. He kept everything in prime working order. He's been gone a few years now, but the stuff was meant to last. He'd roll over in his grave knowing that I was the one who ended up using this place for shelter. He nearly had a stroke when he found us down here, messing with stuff, when we were kids. Told us point-blank that he'd whip our behinds if he ever found us playing in his bunker again."

"Of course you didn't listen, right?"

Jackson summoned the memory and his chest filled with boyish pride. "We went back the very next week, but we were more careful. And he never caught us again."

He brought the flashlight toward Sammie and stood in her ring of light. Her eyes were so wide and pretty right now in the soft glow, but he also found uncertainty in them. She wasn't quite sure she was safe.

"We'll be fine, sweetheart."

"How long do we need to stay down here?" she whispered.

The hatch rattled again, battling against the wind that wanted to shred it to pieces. "I've never seen wind gusts like this. Must be fifty miles an hour. I think we should get comfortable and wait it out. It'll be hours, not minutes, darlin'. Might be all night."

Sammie stared at him. "All night?"

He knew what she was thinking. They were in confined quarters, basically trapped in near darkness. Jackson couldn't let that notion deter him. He had to keep Sammie safe. If it meant spending the night with her in a bunker, they'd manage.

"We should call Tagg or Clay," she said. "To let them know we're down here."

"I'll try. But my battery is almost out and I'm doubting there's reception."

"I'll try my phone." She reached into her purse and a few seconds later let out a little groan. "No reception for me either."

"Winds are interfering with just about everything. The roads are too dangerous to travel anyway. Tagg will know I'll keep you safe, Sammie."

"What about them, Jackson? Is Callie safe up there?"

"Yeah, I think they'll be fine. Tagg is home with her. He won't let anything happen to her."

Sammie was relieved. She prayed Rory did as he was told and stayed put inside his mommy's belly for a little while longer.

"We might as well sit down," Jackson said. He took Sammie's hand to reassure her and made her sit down beside him on the bunk. The old thing creaked but didn't sag as they lowered themselves onto the mattress. He put the flashlight on the floor next to them and set it to the dimmest level to preserve the battery.

Jackson stripped open one slender package and pulled out a Mylar blanket. He wrapped it over Sammie's shoulders and torso and circled his arm around her. "Lay your head on me and try to relax."

She nibbled on her lower lip for a second, and then decided not to argue. With a nod, her head came to rest on his chest. When she spoke, her cool breath tickled his throat. "The two don't go hand in hand, you know. Lying on you and relaxing."

Jackson did know. They were confined together, alone in the dark. Smelling her fresh scent against the stale bunker air and having the side of her breast pressing his underarm wasn't exactly a stroll in the park for him. "You'll be warm soon. The emergency blanket retains body heat."

Sammie snuggled deeper in and, on instinct, Jackson stroked his fingers up and down her arm.

"I think you're giving the blanket too much credit," she murmured.

"Am I?" He looked down at her.

She tilted her head up. Her lips were parted and deliciously close enough to kiss. "Yes."

He summoned his willpower. He wasn't going to take advantage of the situation. Not with Sammie. And it wasn't because of any worry about his brother finding out. It wasn't because Callie would be disappointed in him. He wouldn't touch Sammie tonight because it would be all wrong for her.

"You know, I've got some other ideas about how to have a kick-ass grand opening at Boot Barrage. And because we've got nothing but time tonight, I'd like to run them by you."

He moved his body just enough to keep her small, plump breast from giving him a hard-on and promised himself not to glance at the sweet invitation of her lips.

If he could keep himself from making love to her tonight he would deserve a medal.

Sammie woke to thrashing sounds. Her head lifted from the firm pillow she'd been sleeping on and her eyes popped open. Faint light, earthy scents and loud winds entered her consciousness all at the same time. Her disorientation slowly ebbed until she finally remembered where she was and what had happened.

She was in a bunker, protected from the dust storm outside and sleeping with the sexiest man on earth. Right now she was sprawled across Jackson's body and covered by some space-age material. Her *pillow* was the rock hard wall of his chest. Sammie whimpered and Jackson tightened his hold on her.

Her body went from warm to hot in a flash. They must have dozed for lack of anything better to do. It was late, probably in the wee hours of the night with hours still to go before dawn. She was no longer fearful of the gusting winds attacking the hatch up above and no longer afraid that she might die in a godless sweeping bowl of dust. She was safe with Jackson Worth.

The glimmer of light nearby illuminated part of his handsome face. He had dimples, she knew, but they weren't showing now. Only the sharp angles of his jaw appeared in the shadows. He had beautiful features, that kind of rugged manliness that turned women's heads and made them do stupid things.

Sammie saw beyond Jackson's good looks though. What was it he'd said to her?

I'd like to think I'm more than that.

He was more than that. Tonight was proof of the kind of man he truly was. He'd seen her utter panic in the truck and reassured her. Then he'd found a way out of the storm. He'd protected her with quick action, carrying her from danger to the safety of this shelter.

A deep sigh blew from her lips over Jackson's sleeping form. There was danger, and then there was danger. His arm was still draped over her possessively. Her every nerve ending tingled with awareness as her body pressed against his.

She'd slept with Jackson once before and came away without a clear memory. But her body hadn't forgotten. Her body spoke to her. Cried out in need. She could have lost her life tonight. She might have died and never really known what it was like to be with a man like Jackson Worth. She concentrated on what she wanted, and this time she wouldn't talk sense to herself. This time she let her body give the commands.

And those instincts told her she needed to be with Jackson tonight.

To finally *know* what it was like to make love with him.

She could give herself one night to make a memory rather than be plagued with futile weak images darting in and out of her mind. Her guessing would finally succumb to actual knowledge, and Sammie wanted that beyond all else at this moment.

She brought her finger up to his mouth and traced the outline of his lips. He stirred slightly. Boldly, she lifted her head up to his and without hesitation kissed him with teeny-tiny kisses that wouldn't startle him.

Jackson opened his eyes, the deep midnight-blue irises instantly alighting on her. And she knew the exact moment when he realized that her slender body was partially covering his. Everything below his waist went hard and tight.

Sammie stared into his eyes then, wondering if she'd overstepped her bounds.

He reached behind her head and brought his mouth down on hers. He landed a kiss on her lips that spoke of need and want and powerful desire. When they paused, he whispered in her ear, "Darlin', you want this?"

Sammie was halfway to heaven. She wanted to make the whole trip. She nodded and spoke without hesitation. "Yes."

Oh, yes. She wanted him to take her body and make her his tonight. "Do…you?" she asked.

Jackson ran his hands through the short locks of her hair and looked into her eyes. She held her breath, awaiting his answer. What if he refused her? What if she'd misjudged the entire situation? She would die of mortification and never be able to face him again.

But he didn't give her time to wonder long. He slid his hands down her shoulders, then farther down her lower back and over the slope of her buttocks. Cupping her with both hands, he gave a slight squeeze, a caress of possession that sent shocks of electricity bursting through her body. Next, he positioned her so that the very top of her thighs covered his manhood. His lips parted in a wicked, wicked smile. He spoke quietly but with resolve. "I've been waiting for you to wake up."

Sammie's relief couldn't be greater. She swallowed hard and nodded, suddenly feeling lighter, freer and full of unshed passion. She wouldn't let this night go to waste.

She rubbed her body over Jackson's and made him groan.

"Sweet Sammie," he huffed out with a rasp. "Don't be getting ahead of yourself here."

"I don't want you to change your mind," she whispered. "Or me to change mine."

He reached for her and gave her a kiss that told her what he thought about that. "I'm beyond thinking straight, honey, so no need to worry about that." Then he parted her lips with another kiss and coaxed her tongue with his. How erotic it was to be lying atop Jackson feeling his need consume her in an openmouthed frenzy of kisses. Every touch of his tongue made her quiver below her belly, and every groan of pleasure that escaped his throat made her quivers intensify.

"I want to see you naked again," he said, reaching for her vest. He removed it easily and began unbuttoning her blouse. "I want everything off but your boots."

Sammie's heartbeats nearly pounded out of her chest. He'd seen her naked before, but for the life of her, she couldn't remember it. This time it was new to her and *thrilling*. She wanted to please him as much as she wanted to experience the pleasure he would give her. And he wanted to make love to her with her boots on. "I can do that," she whispered, reaching for his shirt buttons. She wanted to see him naked, too. She wanted to touch him, to explore the firm planes of his muscled chest and the slope of his buttocks, too.

Within seconds, Jackson had her naked but for her Italian suede cuffed boots. She'd barely gotten his shirt off before he'd flipped her onto her back and towered over her. His gaze caressed her with enough heat to burn down the bunker. He was beautifully tanned and muscled in all the right places. She reached up to touch him, to skim her fingers over his chest. To feel his strength and caress a body that was beautiful and perfect.

She laid the flat of her hand on the center of his chest. His heart beat wildly against her palm. How delicious it was to excite a man like Jackson Worth.

"I like when you touch me," he murmured, taking her hand and kissing the tips of her fingers.

"I don't remember any of this," she whispered. "I don't… and I've tried and tried."

He lowered down onto his side next to her and looked her up and down as if he was determining which part of her body he would devour first. She felt suddenly shy, grateful for the low light but turned on by the incredible hunger in his eyes. He brought his mouth down to claim her in a kiss just as his hand cupped her breast. She squirmed from the heady sensation and then moaned when he flattened his palm and rubbed it over the pebbled peak. "I'll make sure you'll remember this time," he said with sweetness in his voice that made her insides melt.

Sammie had no comeback for him. She was speechless, and so much in the Jackson Worth zone that she was already certain she'd never forget a moment of this night.

Her breasts swelled from his attention and when he broke off his kisses and lowered his head, instincts took over and Sammie's body responded to him with hearty welcome. His mouth widened and he suckled her until her cries echoed against the bunker walls. Then he slid his hands down her torso, over her navel and lower still. But he didn't stop where her body ached for him the most. He didn't give her the touch that would send her skyrocketing.

His hands grazed over her thighs and down her legs, caressing her below the knee. He paid all of his attention to her legs, first one, then the other, lifting them up, carressing the sleek moist skin and kissing her there, right where her boots met with the underside of her knees. Sensual spirals curled in her belly and the anticipation of what was to come nearly undid her.

"Jackson," she whimpered with a plea.

He slid his hand up the inside of her thigh, slowly, his fingers pressing the flesh and inching higher to where her need was the greatest. Outside the wind howled and she felt like doing the same.

"Be patient, sweetheart," he rasped in a voice that wasn't all that calm either.

"I need you," she pleaded.

"I'm here," he said, right before his hand found the center of all her need. He put pressure there and Sammie jerked her body, ready to explode.

Jackson stroked her, his fingers finding a sensual rhythm that made her arch and thrust her hips. She rocked back and forth until tiny white hot bursts ignited in her belly, growing with each of his beautifully orchestrated strokes. Little moans of tortured pleasure escaped her lips and she called out his name once, twice. And then she broke apart, shattering with amazing, fast, hot jolts that swept through her belly and clipped her breaths.

"I remember how you respond to me," Jackson said with awe in his voice.

Lying nude, she melted down onto the mattress, feeling languid and sexy, having just been loved so expertly by Jackson. He seemed to know what she needed and had delivered it to her at just the right moment.

She gazed up at his face and watched him take in her body with a potent gleam in his eyes. No matter when or how he looked at her, he always seemed to go back to the same alluring focal point. Her boots.

As soon as he focused on them, the striking blue gleam in his eyes darkened with lust. Her skin prickled from the hot hungry look and Sammie took a big gulp of oxygen.

He touched her shoulders, played with her hair, brought his mouth down to kiss her again and that was all he had to do to spark the dire need that had been temporarily satisfied. Jackson could simply look at her a certain way and she'd grow damp between her legs. "I want more," she said needlessly. Both knew the night was far from over.

Jackson sent her a sweet smile. "You can have all you want."

He removed the rest of his clothes as she watched with eager eyes. There was something extremely appealing about a confident man who wasn't shy about his body. "You can have all you want, too," she whispered.

"I'll take that into consideration, darlin'."

Then he took her into his arms and made love to her as if she was the only woman on earth.

There would be no medals for him tonight. Not even an honorable mention. She'd been sprawled on top of him in her sleep and he hadn't minded breathing in her peachy smells or having her firm breasts squeezed against his chest. He hadn't minded her short caramel strands of hair tickling his chin or her sweet breath caressing his face. Jackson's willpower had vanished with Sammie's first bold yet chaste kisses.

Less than an hour ago, he'd made love to her and after a short respite where he coaxed small talk from her in between snuggling to keep her warm and little pecks on the cheek, they were both ready for the next round. There was no way he could stop himself from taking her again. Her responses to him were too arousing and the situation far too tempting. Sammie had murmured into his ear how much she wanted him again and those sexy words were enough to get him hard and ready for the second time tonight.

She straddled him now, her soft folds of flesh teasing the tip of his manhood, her slender-hipped body upright in the cool air. As she moved, her enticing breasts jiggled. The perfect rosy peaks stood erect, pointing upward. Jackson lay underneath, his hands cupping each side of her buttocks. While he wanted to guide her home, she resisted and played with him, rocking back and forth, whispering over his body with the slightest tease of a touch. His pulse quickened from the erotic way she tormented him until he feared he'd lose it. His groan pierced through the walls of the bunker.

He watched as her eyes took on a glow and her face expressed her deep satisfaction. She was enjoying towering above him, taking charge and calling the shots.

Sammie was something.

Hot.

Sexy.

Erotic.

She had no inhibitions in bed. Not with him anyway. He'd remembered that about her, too.

He couldn't figure how she hadn't married by now. How she hadn't captured a man's heart. She was smart, witty and cute. She looked like an all-American girl, but tonight she was a temptress that any man would find irrestible.

She stopped her torment long enough to hinge forward and take a kiss. He wouldn't let her get away with just one. He wove his hand into her hair and let the loose short locks flow over his fingers. Then he brought her closer, driving his tongue into her mouth and tasting everything female about her. He lavished kiss upon kiss, their tongues doing their own sensual dance.

Her skin was creamy soft and glistening with a silky sheen of moisture as she brushed against him. He lifted her up slightly, lightweight that she was, to kiss her upturned nipples, first one, then the other.

She whimpered her pleasure and his groin turned to stone.

Then he lowered her down on him, fitting her with his pulsing erection until they were joined. The brush of suede made him look down and the vision she made straddling his body, buck-naked except for those damn sexy boots, nearly did him in. He held on, wanting to see Sammie's face when she splintered apart.

She moved on him an inch at a time.

"Damn, Sammie," he gritted out.

"You want more?"

He bucked and filled her fuller. "Ah," she murmured with a sigh.

She rode him harder then, taking him as deep as he could go. Every nerve ending was involved, his body tight and his breathing rapid. Watching her move on him, her slender body finding pace to bring them both to the brink, was a heady intoxication. When he didn't think either could take anymore, he lifted up to circle his arms around her waist. "Ready, darlin'?"

She nodded. She was as far gone as he was. And just before Sammie let herself go, Jackson used his finger to stroke her most sensitive spot until her eyes widened, her mouth went slack and her body went wild. Her response was enough to toss him over the edge. Their breaths huffed out in unison and their thrusting went into overdrive, each giving, each taking, until cries of amazing pleasure tore from their throats. The release was sharp and keen and fulfilling.

Afterward, she collapsed on top of him, her body loose and lazy and well-sated. He brushed a kiss to her forehead, covered her with the blanket and tenderly stroked her arms up and down. She felt soft and malleable and he found that he loved touching her.

Sammie sighed contentedly, and her little sounds stirred him when he thought he'd already died from satisfaction.

"That was awesome," she whispered, her breath tickling his throat.

He smiled. He couldn't agree more.

Her breasts spilled onto his chest and her belly was

pressed against his. Her boot-covered legs were entwined with his, and Jackson seared the memory of making love to her in those boots into his brain. "Yeah."

More rational thoughts occurred to him, too, though. Jackson had to face facts. He'd failed in protecting Sammie from the one thing that could really hurt her. Never mind the dust storm; he shouldn't have taken her tonight. He'd known it all along, but his natural urges and her sweetly wanton ways had him conveniently forgetting who she was and who he was.

He could have a secret fling with Sammie, but that would be foolish and wouldn't end well. But before Jackson could find the right words, Sammie surprised him. "You know what happens in the bunker…"

She didn't have to finish the Vegas slogan for him to get her drift. Jackson aimed a halfhearted smile at her. "I don't kiss and tell, darlin'."

"I'm glad. But since this isn't going to happen again after tonight, ever…" She emphasized the word to make herself clear, then continued in a breathy little voice, "Do you think we can do it again?"

Jackson had had the same idea but he wasn't superhuman. He'd need a little time. "Right now?"

"A little later?" she squeaked out.

He kissed her fully on the lips, hating to disappoint her. "I'm out of condoms, sweetheart."

Through the sliver of light he watched her take a deep breath before blowing it out softly in a faint whisper. "We can make love other ways."

Jackson liked her train of thought. If he had to be trapped in a bunker with a woman, he was glad it was with her. "Now why didn't I think of that?"

She seemed relieved, as if she had feared a refusal.

He tightened his hold on her. "Wake me in half an hour."

"Okay," she said drowsily as she snuggled deeper into his body.

But when the wind stopped howling and finally morning dawned, Sammie was still in his arms, sound asleep under the blanket.

"Sex with Sammie" time had expired.

And it was *time* to face a new day.

It wasn't one minute later that he heard a four-wheel-drive truck pull up. A door slammed and he heard footsteps approaching.

He had a pretty good idea who it was.

"Ah, hell," he muttered.

This was not going to be pretty.

Eight

You don't need lessons in stupid.

Jackson sipped his whiskey slowly while sitting in a Phoenix bar thinking about Tagg's scathing comment at the bunker yesterday morning.

His brother had taken one look at Jackson coming out of the bunker and had known that he'd had a wild night of sex. He hadn't had time to button his shirt or run a hand through his rumpled hair in his rush to keep his brother from knocking on the hatch door and startling Sammie awake. At the very least he'd saved her the embarrassment of facing Tagg.

The rest of their conversation had gone downhill, with Jackson getting an earful about Tagg's concern with their safety and how worried he and Callie had been about the both of them. Tagg had lowered his voice then and reamed Jackson out about Sammie's vulnerability and how she needed stability in her life.

Jackson's blood had boiled, but he couldn't disagree with

his brother. Making love to Sammie wasn't a bright move on his part, but damn it all, it hadn't felt like a mistake.

It had taken all of Jackson's skills of persuasion to get Tagg to leave the scene and agree not to tell Callie about this. If Sammie chose to tell her, that was another matter. But his brother had left him with a parting message. "I'm gonna forget about this, but don't mess with Sammie. Not unless she means something important to you."

Jackson polished off his drink and flagged the bartender down for another. He was two sips into it when Blair Caulfield slid onto the bar stool next to him. "Sorry I'm late."

"It's okay," he said. He wasn't looking forward to this meeting.

Every male head in the bar turned to look at her. She was something to see, in a slinky body-hugging dress piled with tiny silver sequins that glimmered in the bar light. A diamond necklace graced her long beautiful neck and honey-blond hair flowed past her shoulders in waves.

"Did you miss me?"

He gazed into her summer sky-blue eyes. "Maybe once upon a time."

"I'm a different woman now," she said defensively.

"And I'm not the man you once knew."

Her size 38 bust—if he knew women—nearly spilled out of the dress as she let go a breathy little sigh. "Jackson, I didn't know you as a man. You were a boy and I was a girl."

He shrugged. "Whatever, Blair," he said, gesturing for the bartender to come over.

She gave him her order with a smile, flashing her eyes. Jackson realized Blair couldn't help being sexy and alluring. It came as naturally to her as breathing. She drew men to her like a magnet.

Jackson recognized that quality and, to his amazement, realized he might be looking at a female version of himself.

He blinked.

She touched his arm, running her fingertips over his shirt. "Remember when we would go down to the lake and toss pebbles? We made a game out of it."

It was one of the good memories. "I let you win most times."

Her eyes took on a glow. "I know. That's what I loved about you. You put my feelings above your own."

Jackson had loved her to distraction. And she'd broken his heart in a thousand different ways.

"You may not believe this, but you were the first and last man to do that for me. With you, I had everything and I was too foolhardy to know it back then."

"You win some and you lose some, Blair."

"Jackson," she said in a sweet pleading tone that also conjured good memories, "won't you cut me some slack? I'm trying to make it up to you."

He heaved his chest in a silent sigh. She was getting to him. And it bugged the manure out of him. "Are you ready for dinner?"

She glanced at the cosmopolitan she hadn't touched and nodded. "Yes. Let's have dinner."

Half an hour later they sat facing each other in an upscale Scottsdale restaurant, eating filet mignon and drinking a fine California Sauvignon. Jackson wanted only one thing from Blair Caulfield and he wondered if she knew it. Surely old Pearson would have told her how much he'd wanted that strip of land when she'd purchased it. He wracked his brain trying to figure out how Blair convinced the old man to sell her his property.

Finally, after listening to Blair's small talk, Jackson had had enough. "So, how'd you do it, Blair? How'd you get Pearson to sell you his land?"

Blair didn't bat an eyelash or pretend not to know what he was talking about. "I can't tell you."

"You can't. Or won't?"

"Both, really."

"Even you wouldn't seduce that ole codger to get ahold of his property, or would you?"

She jerked back, her eyes snapping with surprise as if his comment wasn't so much insulting as it was obscene. It took her a few seconds to recover.

Then with a polished smile, one she forced onto her face, she continued, "The fact is I own that land now. And there are two very motivated buyers for that piece of property. I haven't decided what I want to do with it."

She lowered her lashes for a second and then lifted her beautiful face to his. *"Yet."*

She could either sell the land to real estate developers, or sell it to him. Jackson's didn't want to play by her rules. Not tonight. He had too many other things on his mind. "There're three people dead because they weren't lucky enough to be in the right place at the right time yesterday. That dust storm caused this city a world of hurt and you're still oblivious to life around you. You're still playing games."

Her face reddened at his accusation but her voice was eerily calm. "You're right here with me, Jackson. Eating steak."

Jackson leaned forward, angry at her and at himself. He'd been batting zero with women lately. First Sammie, his business partner and family friend who he couldn't get off his mind, and now Blair, his self-centered ex-girlfriend. "Worth Enterprises set up an emergency station for anyone that needed help today. We had food and water and transportation for people who needed it. I can eat my meal without guilt."

"I can, too. I donated twenty thousand dollars to the local Red Cross today to lend a hand."

Jackson twisted his lips and nodded. He was being unduly hard on Blair and she took his abuse without retreating. "Then I stand corrected."

She toyed with her goblet of wine, giving him a hopeful look that reminded him of the younger Blair, the one he'd fallen in love with before greed and wanderlust had changed her. "Are you giving me a pat on the back?"

"Isn't that what you want?"

"No,' she whispered. "I want more than that from you. I want a second chance."

They stared at each other a long time. He couldn't let her sell off the land that should belong to the Worths. Or believe her when she claimed she wanted him back. If she had meant it and had truly changed her ways, she wouldn't be resorting to blackmail to get into his good graces. Yet, for a second there, he'd seen the girl he'd once loved.

"It's been a long day, Blair." He'd cancelled all of his appointments and his office staff helped him set up a donation center for the dust storm victims, where they handed out bottles of water, granola bars and fresh fruit and offered rides for those who had lost their transportation.

"I know. And a hard one. We could go back to your place and *relax*," she suggested, crossing her arms and leaning forward so that her cleavage squeezed tight. The move had men at other tables glancing over.

"You don't even know whether I'm involved with someone."

Her eyes grew wide, as if the thought just dawned on her. "Are you?"

The image of Sammie cuddled under a blanket in the bunk bed fast asleep after he'd made love to her immediately flashed into his mind. "No."

She batted her eyes at him again. "We could forget the past, Jackson, and start new."

She thought she wanted him back, but Jackson knew she was deceiving herself. He wouldn't let her deceive him for a second time.

"We'll do it another time."

She took another sip of wine and eyed him carefully with just the right touch of softness in her expression. "Are you stringing me along?"

"Funny, I was going to ask you the same thing."

Sammie ran her hand along the smooth Italian leather of a pair of Sergio Rossi boots. The short boots' hidden zippers and bladelike stiletto heels made this design a favorite. She placed them carefully on a Plexiglas stand, arranging them just so, and then took a step back to view her display. It was the icing on the cake. "Nice."

Boot Barrage was now fully repaired from the fire and filled with shabby chic shelving, tables, overhead lighting and more than two hundred different styles of boots. She had an area designed for working women named WW, with more comfortable, low-heeled boots that were studded, cuffed or zippered for style and wear. Her Night On the Town area was especially designed for women who wanted to make a statement on a hot date. That part of the store was lit with spotlights on select designer boots that deserved star treatment. Sunset Soles was a section to the right she'd appropriately named for a line of western boots that would take lots of wear and tear on the range or ranch. And Deals on High Heels was off to the left toward the back of the store. It sounded much better than bargain basement, or clearance rack. She'd priced those boots to sell as a loss leader to stimulate sales. The store had something for everyone's style and taste.

In the very back of the boutique she'd installed an upscale lounge with a coffee machine that provided café mocha, cappuccino and hot chocolate. Fresh pastries would be served tomorrow for the grand opening and then she'd be in business. Literally.

With a sense of accomplishment Sammie glanced around Boot Barrage, grateful for this second chance and grateful to be alive. She had Jackson to thank for both of those gifts and she didn't dare dream of anything more.

She was still recovering from the dust storm and the storm that was Jackson Worth. The wall of dust had scared her silly. She'd never seen anything like it in her life. The horrendous monster coming at them had looked like a low-budget sci-fi movie with bad special effects. But the reality of the destruction that lay in its wake was all too close for comfort. Red Ridge residents had gone back to life as normal as far as she knew. Still, the destruction had left some homeless and some without electrical power and it had killed others. She shivered at the thought.

As for Jackson, she'd only seen him a few times since the dust storm and when they'd been together it was to talk about the opening and go over details. He'd acted as though nothing had happened between them, just as she'd asked. He'd taken the famous "what happens in Vegas" slogan to heart by her own request and they'd both pretended they hadn't ripped up the sheets in that bunker that night.

Jackson was pretty hard to forget and she had a fantastic memory to take to her grave. Another slogan came to mind: we'll always have Paris. And she'd always have *the bunker*.

"Sammie, you are ridiculous," she muttered to herself.

She was. But she was thrilled about her accomplishments with Boot Barrage, and that overshadowed everything else in comparison.

"What's ridiculous?"

Jackson came toward her, weaving his way around her displays to the front of the store, where she'd been busy giving herself mental accolades. "Oh, nothing. I didn't hear you come in."

He reached her and scanned the entire boutique with sharp eyes. "This place looks great."

"Thanks. I had help. Angie is doing a great job. She's helped me get this place stocked and organized."

"I'm glad she's working out for you."

In the end, after all that business about who would lead the interviews for part-time help, Jackson had given up the reins to her. "And Nicole is sharp as a tack working the cash register."

Both of the girls she'd hired were going to college at Arizona State University, and had flexible schedules. Both were intelligent and personable and needed a paycheck. With the three of them, Sammie was sure they'd manage okay.

"What's up?" Sammie asked.

Lately it wasn't like Jackson to show up unannounced. Instead of his usual dark stone-washed jeans or business suit, today he wore cut-off gray sweats, a black tank top and tennis shoes. The bronzed muscles in his arms popped under the lights. Sammie couldn't ignore a man like Jackson, so she didn't even try. She was sort of helpless in that department and he was most likely used to women ogling him.

"Nothing much. Just making sure you've got everything ready for tomorrow."

"I think I've got it under control," she said with a happy sigh.

He glanced at the very serviceable boots she wore today and arched a brow. "Were you wearing boots the first time I met you?"

She took a moment to think about it. "You mean at Callie and Tagg's wedding?"

"Yeah."

"No. I didn't bring any along. It was all pretty rushed on my end to get to Red Ridge in time."

Her answer seemed to satisfy his curiosity and he gave her a nod.

But the mention of her boots brought back images of her naked body joined with his as they both moaned their way to heaven. Her nerve endings tingled in response. She'd never forget the sated look on Jackson's face after she'd ridden him hard wearing her gray suede cuffed boots. Nor could she imagine wearing those boots anywhere else ever again for fear sensual memories would surface at inopportune moments.

Her discomfort was interrupted by a knock on the front door. It was Sonny Estes.

Before she could get to the door, Jackson was there, pulling it open. The two men shook hands. Then Sonny turned to her. "Hey, beautiful."

Warmth filled her cheeks. He'd started calling her that after she'd agreed to run with him in the mornings. And she'd decided to do that right after the night she'd spent in the bunker with Jackson. "Hi, Sonny."

He did a quick scan of the finished store. "The place looks *muy* fantastic." He'd visited the boutique a few times, catching her when she was alone to view the progress, but he hadn't seen it completed.

She laughed. "Thanks." And then she noticed he was dressed in much the same way Jackson was, in shorts and a tank. "You guys off somewhere?"

"Sonny's a glutton for punishment," Jackson said, teasing. "Seems he's got a freezer full of ice cream he needs to unload."

"Ah, basketball." She was glad they'd both be out of her hair. She had last-minute things she wanted to do. "Well, have a nice time."

Jackson sent his friend a smile. "You get the feeling she wants to *boot* us out of here?"

Sammie rolled her eyes.

Sonny laughed. "Will I see you tomorrow morning, same as usual?" he asked. "Or am I losing my partner when this place opens?"

"Oh, uh…I can probably manage both. I'll be too keyed up in the morning to sleep anyway."

Jackson shot her a pointed look. "What are you talking about?"

His tone held a slight edge. Sammie hesitated. She didn't have anything to hide, but she hadn't mentioned her morning jogs to Jackson, and now he appeared extremely interested in her answer.

"Sammie and I run together every morning," Sonny volunteered. "Just after dawn."

Jackson's eyes flickered and he aimed an icy glare at his friend for just an instant. Then his face transformed to the Jackson everyone knew and loved. "You don't say?"

"I can barely keep up with Sonny but he takes pity on me."

"I bet he does." Jackson blinked a few times.

Sammie wouldn't read too much into it. Jackson wasn't the jealous type. He had too much going for him to worry about who she might be jogging with in the mornings.

"You ready, Jack?" Sonny said.

"Yeah, I'll meet you outside."

He gave Sammie and her boots a once over as soon as Sonny walked out. Then he bent his head so close she thought he might kiss her. "Seems you have a lot of secrets, Sammie."

"Not that many." And most of them are with you, she wanted to say. "Well, you'd better go. The ball's in your court," she added, unable to resist. "Or whatever that saying is."

Jackson's eyes flickered. Did he know she was baiting him? He was too smart not to know, she decided. And as she watched him walk out the door, she gave herself a mental pat on the back. For once she'd had the last word with Jackson.

Jackson took great pleasure in squashing Sonny's game on the court. He racked up three three-point shots in a row and had dominated their one-on-one match up. Wiping sweat from his brow, he walked over to the front bench of the bleachers to take a break. Overhead lights atop tall steel posts beamed down and Jackson barely felt the cool chill in the night air any longer. He was heated, and he figured it wasn't just from the game. He grabbed a bottle of water and emptied half of it in one big gulp.

"Man, you're harsh tonight," Sonny said, coming over. He sat down, stretched his legs and leaned back against the bleachers, twisting the cap off a bottle of water.

Jackson had been a jock in high school and knew how to compete when it mattered. Tonight it seemed to matter more than usual.

"I didn't think you were into Sammie." Sonny looked at him before taking a swig.

Jackson shook his head, his brows gathering. "What?"

"You heard me." He gestured toward the court. "You've got more than basketball on your mind, my friend. You were playing with a vengeance. What's up?"

"Nothing's up." He waved him off.

"You mean I'm plumb *loco?*" Sonny gave his best John Wayne impression.

"Speaking in Old West terms, yeah, you're plumb loco."

"Okay, then if that's the case, you won't mind if I ask Sammie out, right?"

Jackson finished off his drink and set the bottle down, giving Sonny a long, serious look. "I don't mind."

Sonny laughed right in his face. "Man, you're in major denial. You're into Sammie."

He shook his head and told a bald-faced lie. "She's not my type."

The truth was, Sammie appealed to him in ways he didn't understand. The boot thing made no sense either. He was still trying to figure that one out.

Sonny's mouth twisted with disbelief. "Wonder what she'd say about that."

Jackson was through playing head games with his friend. He gritted his teeth, his temper balancing precariously on edge. It took a lot to make Jackson angry. He was usually a cool customer who couldn't be rattled, but Sonny was getting under his skin. Jackson had a protective streak when it came to Sammie. He didn't want anyone to hurt her. *No, you're saving that privilege for yourself.* "You're not telling Sammie a thing."

"If you say so." Sonny didn't sound too convincing. "But if you're not interested, move aside and give someone else a chance."

"I'm not standing in your way."

"Didn't look that way when you found out I'm jogging with her."

"No big deal."

"Sammie noticed, too. It was hard not to see your jaw drop to the ground."

"What's your point?"

"She's nice and a lot of fun. I'd like a chance to get to know her better."

"Go to hell," Jackson said mildly. Sammie was off-limits to Jackson, but that didn't mean that she was fair game for

Sonny. "Or better yet, let's get back on the court and I'll take you there personally."

After the game, Jackson dropped Sonny off at Sonny Side Up and noticed that the lights to the boutique were still on. The devil in him had him turning his car around and parking in the lot in the back. He picked up his cell phone and dialed Sammie's number. "I'm here."

"Nice of you to warn me," Sammie said.

He smiled and used his key to go inside. Sammie was sitting at her small desk in the office, her head down going over paperwork. She didn't bother to look up. "I'm just about finished here," she said, making a notation on an invoice.

She glanced at him then, and the pen she was holding dropped out of her hand. Her gaze caressed his sweaty, glistening shoulders and she took a swallow. "You should put your shirt on. It's cold out there."

He took a step closer and her fruity, fresh scent invaded his nostrils. One look at her super non-sexy boots had him mentally cursing. They still turned him upside down.

Sammie stayed glued to her seat, her hands clutching the sides of the chair as if she were hanging on for dear life. "How was your game?"

"Invigorating."

She put her head down again, pretending interest in her invoices. Short blades of caramel hair framed her face. "I can see that."

"Sammie," he said, unable to stop himself. He didn't like being baited and both Sonny and Sammie had managed it tonight.

She picked up her pen and began writing something down on her notepad. "Did you forget something?"

"Yeah, you could say that."

Her pretty brown eyes went wide when he hoisted her to her feet and draped both arms around her waist, pulling her close. He liked how her hands automatically circled his shoulders. Holding her brought back memories of Vegas and the bunker, especially when her sweet body went pliant the second he touched her. His mouth hovered close to hers and their breaths mingled. "I forgot to wish you luck tomorrow."

And then he sipped from her lips, slowly, deliberately, drinking in the sweet taste of café mocha and cherry lip gloss. She was so damn giving as if her mouth was made for his. He kissed her a second time for added luck and then opened his eyes, glancing over her shoulder at the three words she'd written sandwiched between penned-in stars on the notepad.

Remember the pact

It was a cold splash of water to his libido and his conscience. He didn't feel guilty for kissing her though and that was his only consolation as he set her aside. He cleared his throat and took a step back. "I think that does it, darlin'."

"We should have a windfall tomorrow," she said, touching the spot where he'd just kissed her. "After that good luck kiss."

She always had a comeback. Her sparring kept him on his toes. "I'll be by later in the day tomorrow to see how it's going."

Her mouth turned down. "You're not coming in the morning?"

He didn't have to glance at the note again to be reminded of his commitment and his pledge. He'd broken his word—something a Worth didn't do—enough times with Sammie. He had to regard the note she'd written down on that pad as a plea…a way to keep them both on track. "You and the girls will handle it. It's your shop, Sammie, and I have faith in your abilities."

It was best this way, Jackson told himself. He'd done what

he could to see that Boot Barrage got off to a good start. He walked out the door with new determination and a lump of doubt clogging his throat as he let Sammie go.

Nine

"Thank you, Mrs. Elroy," Sammie said, handing Betty Lou Elroy's niece a glossy white shopping bag with Boot Barrage's delicately scripted double B insignia on the face. "I hope you enjoy the boots. And remember, our special Gold service is available to you whenever you want to shine them up or need assistance in any other way."

"Thank you, ma'am. And everyone always calls me Lindsay," the young woman said sweetly. "I'll be sure to come back soon. I've got my eye on a few other pairs over there."

Sammie smiled. "They'll be here waiting for you."

Sammie walked Lindsay out and greeted another woman as she entered the boutique. In the two hours since they'd opened the doors, Boot Barrage had had a steady flow of customers. Many came to browse and have a pastry or two, and some sipped lattes and simply inquired about Sammie and how she came to open a store in Scottsdale. Others came to buy. Sammie spent equal time with everyone, getting to know her would-be clients with a friendly smile and gracious attitude.

Every time she heard Nicole open the cash drawer, her heart sang. Sales were going great from word of mouth, her flyers and ads in local papers. The Worths' influence in town couldn't be overlooked either. The last three sales had been from someone from within the Worths' circle.

Along with Lindsay, Ellen Branford, the married daughter of Clayton's ranch manager, exited the store wearing her new purchase, a pair of tan leather riding boots. Kyra Muldoon, Tagg's first wife's cousin, walked out with two pairs from the Deals on High Heels table along with a pair of single-studded ankle boots.

Sammie had a chance to meet some of Scottsdale's elite women, some sweet, others high and mighty, but all interested in Boot Barrage and what the store had to offer.

As the afternoon rolled around, there was a lull in the flow of traffic. Sammie had given Angie her lunch break and Nicole was in the stock room checking on inventory when a stunning woman sauntered in, her long wavy blond hair flowing neatly over a sleek black bolero jacket, tight capris that gave definition to the shapely slope of her derriere and tall, spiky sandals that made Sammie wonder how she kept her balance. The woman wore a string of diamonds around her throat that added just the right touch to the ensemble without being gaudy.

"Hello and welcome to Boot Barrage. I'm Sammie Gold," she said, greeting her new customer.

The woman nodded, her gaze scanning the boutique briskly, taking it all in. She barely seemed to notice Sammie as she introduced herself. "Blair Caulfield."

Sammie froze for an instant. Something powerful slammed into her gut as the blonde gave her a small smile.

She was *the* Blair Caulfield, the destroyer of men. Of one man, Sammie corrected herself.

"Lovely shop," she said. "I'll pick up a few pairs of boots on my way out."

Sammie hesitated, nibbling on her lip. "On your way out?"

"Yes, but first I'd like to see Jackson Worth. Your employer. Is he here?" She glanced around the room with perfectly made-up blue eyes that looked like summer skies and the deep sea at the same time.

Her automatic assumption that Jackson was Sammie's boss struck her like fingernails scraping on a chalkboard. Sammie kept her wits and quashed a frown. The woman was beautiful, obviously wealthy and obtusely ignorant. "Jackson is my partner. We are in business *together*," she took great joy in announcing, "and he's not here."

"He will be soon." She finally gave Sammie her full attention, leveling her with those baby blues. "I'm meeting him here."

"Oh…I see." Raw jealousy ate its way through Sammie's good nature. She could still practically taste Jackson's good-luck kiss on her lips. With her heart in her throat, she struggled for civility. "Well, you can shop while you wait for him." At least she could take some of the woman's money.

"I think I will. He's worth the wait, if you know what I mean." She gave Sammie a direct look, then batted her eyes.

"I'm sure I don't," Sammie lied openly, her sense of pride getting in the way of the truth. Then she thought better of it. She shouldn't allow this woman to get to her. "Actually, let me correct that. I *do* know."

Blair cocked her head to one side and sent Sammie a condescending smile with a slow shake of the head. "You've fallen for him, haven't you? It's hard not to," she said, making that notion seem pitiable. "He's better looking now than when he was a boy. But don't waste your time. I've come back to claim what's mine. And Jackson has always been mine."

Her words hit like a cold, insulting blast. The last thing Sammie wanted was a verbal battle, but she couldn't let Blair get away with that. "I wonder if that's true anymore. Jackson is his own man."

"I don't doubt it. But I have something Jackson wants," she informed Sammie. "And I'm the only one who can give it to him."

Sammie steeled herself. She wasn't going to allow Blair Caulfield to walk into Boot Barrage's grand opening and ruin her day. She had worked too darn hard for this. And when she thought about it, Jackson deserved better than Blair Caulfield.

But it was truly none of her business. What was her business was making sales and building a clientele today. She wasn't Jackson's protector or his girlfriend. Actually, she'd never known how to label their relationship.

"If you'll excuse me, I have another customer."

Sammie left Blair to her own devices, which ended up being lucrative sales for Boot Barrage. Jackson's old love had expensive taste. She purchased three pairs of the most stylish high-priced boots in the shop. Luckily, after waiting a while, Blair got an urgent phone call and had to leave immediately, asking Sammie to have Jackson call her later.

When pigs fly, Sammie thought.

Two hours later, Jackson walked into the boutique bringing along with him a very pregnant Callie, Tagg and Trish. She met them by the coffee lounge. "Welcome!" She hugged Trish and Tagg, then took more care in embracing Callie, whose baby belly looked exceedingly enormous today. "Thanks for coming, all of you."

"The place looks beautiful," Callie said, her voice filled with pride. "I love it."

"I can't believe you made the trip here for the opening."

Callie gave her a reassuring squeeze of the hand. "I wouldn't miss it. I wanted to surprise you."

"You have." Sammie's eyes misted up. It meant the world to her to have her best friend here today. She hadn't seen Callie since the night of the dust storm. They'd talked at length afterward about the ordeal and Sammie never did get up the nerve to tell her what had happened between her and Jackson. Right now it felt like the right decision, especially after Miss-Jackson's-Mine-and-I-Have-What-He-Wants showed up.

Since Blair had left an hour ago, Sammie's mood had lifted considerably.

"You can thank Jackson for me being here," Callie said. "He convinced Tagg that I could travel. You know Tagg's overly—"

"Nervous is what I am," Tagg said. "My wife is ready to pop."

"I am not," Callie said, laying a loving hand on her belly. "And there'll be plenty of time to get to the hospital when the baby decides to come," she reassured him.

Tagg didn't look convinced, but he relented. "I'm holding my brother responsible for his lack of judgment."

Jackson glanced at Callie's belly and fear entered his eyes. "Stay in there, Rory, or your Uncle Jackson will be tarred and feathered and kicked out of town."

Everyone laughed, including Tagg.

"Well, I'm glad you're all here," Sammie said. Her heart melted a little in appreciation of Jackson's efforts to bring Callie here. It meant a lot to her.

Trish looked over the shop. "I like what you've done here.

It's elegant, intimate and functional. That's hard to achieve all at once. Your displays look fantastic."

"Thank you. I'm pretty proud of it myself. But Jackson had a hand in making this happen."

Callie smiled. "It's what he does best."

No, it wasn't what he did the very best, but Sammie held that thought hostage.

Jackson took the high road. "Sammie designed the place from top to bottom. I only added my two cents here and there."

More like tens of thousands of dollars, but Sammie wouldn't correct him.

She spent the next ten minutes showing off the facility and introducing the Worths to Angie and Nicole, who'd been eager to meet the rest of the clan. Both girls were raised on Clayton Worth's music and were a tiny bit disappointed Clay had decided to stay home with little Meggie, who was teething and cranky.

After her friends left, Jackson stayed behind. It felt right having him here to help close the shop. Not that he was doing much other than following her around as she straightened out the shelves, arranged the boots and finally locked the front door. She glanced at her watch. Seven o'clock. It felt like midnight.

"Oh, I almost forgot. Blair Caulfield was here today. Looking for you. I was to deliver the message for you to call her."

Jackson didn't say a word, instead taking keen interest in a tall pair of inky leather boots with open toes and straps that crisscrossed all the way to the knee. Only a wide strip of material running up the back of the leg held them together. They were the latest fashion and were described as boots for lack of a better term. The designer had named them after his beloved wife, Marianna. Mariannas only came in one color, black, and Sammie couldn't figure out if they were derived from Grecian sandals or had something to do with bondage. Either way, Jackson seemed intrigued.

"Blair's a beautiful woman," Sammie said, "although I doubt her IQ rallies over double digits."

Jackson finally looked at her. "She's old news."

"She doesn't think so."

"That's her problem, isn't it?"

Sammie was way too relieved to hear him say that. "Maybe she needs clarification."

Jackson took up looking at the boots again.

The subject was closed. It wasn't her business anyway, she reminded herself. She went about tidying up the last of the tables in silence.

"Let's go to dinner," Jackson said after a minute, "to celebrate day one."

She was too tired. And weak. She didn't think she could stand to be with her deadly handsome, not-a-hair-out-of-place, six-foot-two hunk of a business partner for a cozy dinner tonight. In his usual cowboy attire—dark jeans, silver belt buckle and a studded cobalt-blue western shirt that brought out the fascinating hue of his eyes—Jackson could easily make mush of her resolve.

She shook her head. "Can I take a rain check? My feet are killing me. I can't wait to get undressed and relax, but first I want to go over the books."

"Aren't you hungry?" He asked as they worked their way to the back of the store. He scoured the empty pastry table and fiddled with the coffee machine that Angie had shut down before she left for the day. "There's nothing to eat here. I bet you didn't have lunch today."

"I, uh…come to think of it, I didn't. I guess I forgot."

"Making all those sales."

"You're darn tootin'."

Jackson grinned. "Well, c'mon in here," he said, leading the way into the office. "I'll help you go over the books and call for Chinese."

"I want barbecue."

"Okay, Miss Picky, I'll order barbecue and after we check sales, you can go home, tuck yourself into bed and have good dreams."

"Sounds like a plan," Sammie said, realizing that Jackson Worth was her friend.

For some odd reason, that thought depressed her.

In the wee hours of the following Monday morning, Sammie's phone rang, waking her from a sound sleep. Prying her eyes open, she leaned over and fumbled for the phone on the nightstand. "Hello," she whispered, fuzzy-brained.

"Are you ready to be a godparent?"

Jackson's deep voice registered as she turned on the light. "Wha…oh." She sat straight up in bed. "Callie?"

"She's in labor. Just got a call from Tagg. Everyone's heading to the hospital in Red Ridge now."

"Wow, it's really happening. Okay. I'll get dressed and head over—"

"I'll pick you up. We'll drive out together."

Sammie couldn't deny that this time the "we" sounded good to her ears. She was still half asleep, and thinking of Callie and the baby's arrival made her a little jittery and nervous. It would be a relief to have Jackson chauffeur her to Red Ridge. "Okay, give me a few minutes."

"Pack a bag. I'm almost at your door."

"You're not serious."

"I'm always serious when it comes to my nephew's birth."

Sammie hung up the phone and rushed into the shower, the speediest way she knew to wake herself up quickly. It was two-fifteen in the morning and having to move fast at this hour was a chore. Yet less than ten minutes later she was ready when Jackson knocked on her front door. "Thanks for the notice."

"I knew you could do it." He grinned, flashing perfect teeth on a face sporting five-o'clock shadow verging on early-morning stubble. Of course, on Jackson, it didn't look scruffy at all but sexy as sin. She sighed. There was no denying he was the beautiful one in this duo.

She slung a running bag she'd managed to pack with a few essentials and a change of clothes over her shoulder. Labor could take an hour or it could take days. However long it did take, Sammie wanted to be there to support Callie and greet little Rory in person when he made his first appearance in the world.

Jackson ushered her out of her apartment, closing her door and guiding her with a hand to the small of her back. She got into his king-cab truck and tossed her bag in the back. "Drive, Uncle Jackson. And I hope you brought coffee."

He lifted a silver Thermos. "Yes, your majesty."

She managed a chuckle and took the coffee from him, sipping from the opened lid. After a few sips, he glanced at her. "I didn't take you for a coffee hog."

"I am." She sipped some more.

"Hand it over. I need caffeine to stay awake."

So not true. He was as alert as they come. Sammie noticed things like that. Jackson always had a plan. He was always sharp as a tack. He never let anyone get the best of him.

She gazed down at the steam rising from the canister in her hand. They'd shared meals, faced near death and slept together more than once, but oddly, the thought of sharing the same individual-sized Thermos of coffee with him seemed incredibly intimate.

Their fingers brushed as she handed it over. She was getting used to having him touch her, but by no means had her responses dulled. Still, each and every time he laid a hand on her, bombshells went off inside.

He kept his eyes on the road and sipped from where her lips had just been. "Thanks."

"Uh-huh. Just don't drink it all. I still have some waking up to do."

He turned on the radio. Tim McGraw's voice blasted into the night. Jackson kept Sammie from dozing by humming off tune.

They arrived at the small private hospital in Red Ridge well before dawn and found Trish and Clay in the waiting room. "Tagg's been with her the whole time," Trish said.

"How is she?" Sammie asked.

"She's doing pretty well. Her water broke after midnight. She's having good contractions and trying to have a natural birth. It's been a few hours and she hasn't changed her mind yet."

"Where's little Meggie?" Jackson asked.

"At home with Helen." The Worth housekeeper was more like a relative, having been with the family for more than twenty years. "Sound asleep."

Jackson nodded and walked over to where Clay was standing.

Sammie had no experience with childbirth. She had few friends who'd had children, so this was all new to her. She settled onto a chair next to Trish. They conversed for a little while and that helped Sammie's jumpy nerves to relax a little. The bright hospital lights and the realization that a new life was about to come into the world kept her more alert than the leaded coffee she'd had earlier.

After a few minutes of baby talk, Trish changed the subject. "Who's minding the store tomorrow?" she asked. Trish had been in business most of her adult life. She'd once been

Clay's publicist and they'd almost divorced before realizing that their love could conquer any obstacle that came their way. Sammie thought it a romantic notion.

"Oh, my godson is a genius. He decided to arrive on my day off. We're closed on Mondays."

Trish chuckled. "That *is* pretty good timing. Rory gets props for that. And I know how badly Callie wanted you to be here."

"I wouldn't be anywhere else. Even if it meant closing up shop for a few days. Boot Barrage got off to a good start. We're on the map, as they say."

"From what I could tell, you'll do well. It's a great location. And you've got a sound business partner. Jackson is very capable."

He was a gazillionaire who'd made most of his money using his brains and talent. Sammie had been given a gift having Jackson as a partner. She looked up, and their eyes met from across the waiting room for one long stretched-out moment before Jackson took up pacing the marble floor with Clay again. "I know," she said quietly.

Half an hour later Tagg came in search of Sammie. "She wants you to come in."

Sammie rose immediately and followed him through heavy beige double doors and down a hallway that led to the labor room. Callie started having a contraction the minute Sammie spotted her, and Tagg rushed to one side to hold her hand and coach her breathing. Sammie came to the other side of her bed to take the other hand. "I'm here."

Callie nodded, concentrating on taking slow easy breaths. The sheets were tossed off and Callie wore a functional green-and-white hospital gown. The room had low soothing lights and a nurse nearby spoke in hushed tones.

Callie gave Tagg every ounce of her concentration as she made it through the contraction. When it was over, she sat up a little straighter in the bed and turned to Sammie. "I'm glad to see you."

"Me, too." Sammie brushed aside a lock of hair that had slipped onto Callie's damp forehead. "How're you doing?"

"Managing so far."

"I can see that. You're a trouper. I can't wait to meet Rory."

"He'll be here soon," she said. "He wants out."

"That's a good thing. He wants to greet his mom and dad."

"I can't believe I'm going to be a mother," Callie confessed. "It's hard to imagine that just months ago, Tagg and I weren't even speaking to each other and now he's my husband and the father of my child."

Tagg kissed her cheek. "It took some doing, but I'm glad of it."

"So am I," Callie said with love in her eyes.

Callie squeezed both of their hands at the same time. "Oh, I think another one is coming."

Sammie looked at the fetal monitor screen recording the labor and watched the indicator begin to rise. "Wow, no fooling. Hang on," she said.

A little while after that the doctor announced that it was time for Callie to push. Sammie gave her friend an encouraging look and blew her a kiss before she walked out the door to give the rest of the family the news.

Less than an hour later Tagg wore a smile of relief as he entered the waiting room. "Little Rory wants to meet his family."

He was met with handshakes and congratulations and then each one of the Worths filed into the postpartum room where Callie was recovering. She looked good. The color was restored to her cheeks and she was wearing a contented expression not even Hawk Sullivan, Callie's difficult, stern father, could wipe away. He walked into the room looking sheepish, holding a bouquet of roses for Callie and a powder-blue teddy bear for his grandson.

Tagg sat down on the bed holding a very red-faced, papoose-wrapped bundle in his arms.

It was a time to celebrate and thank God for the blessing of a healthy child. Everyone took turns greeting Rory and the brave ones held the little boy in their arms.

When Jackson sat down on a rocking chair and put out his arms to hold Rory no one was more surprised than Sammie. Tagg bent low and carefully set his new son into the cradle of Jackson's arms. He held the baby carefully and close to his chest, whispering sweet words of love to him with an expression of awe, pride and protection.

Something sharp, powerful and *painful* stabbed Sammie in the heart.

It was a one-minute interlude, a brief span of time that Jackson held his godson, but in that moment Sammie recognized an emotion coming freely, naturally and without fanfare.

She was in love with Jackson Worth.

And it wasn't his deadly good looks, his incredible charm or even having wild times in bed with him that brought her feelings front and center. No, it was just this one simple act of love. One simple gesture. One simple display of the man Jackson truly was, that snuck its way in and gave a blunt twist to her gut.

She'd always thought true love would hit like a jolt, a lightning blast, fireworks that brightened the dark sky. But what she felt for Jackson had sort of crawled its way inside and invaded quietly, despite her attempts to keep a safe distance away.

She'd told herself a hundred times that he wasn't the man for her. His confirmed bachelorhood, his own admission that he didn't want to hurt her, their secret pact—all of that was instantly nullified the second Jackson picked up his godson and nuzzled him to his chest.

That's all it had taken for her to realize the truth.

Momentary joy had entered her heart at loving him, but now that emotion was dwarfed by something looming larger—the knowledge that Jackson would never be hers. Not in the way she wanted him. Not in the way that mattered.

She loved him.

But she'd never again settle for something less than what Callie had with Tagg. Or what Trish had with Clay. She wanted Jackson's love and commitment. And even as that became clear, she also realized it was an impossible dream.

"Would you like to hold your godson?" Jackson asked, rising from the rocker.

He stood beside her and as they made the cautious transfer, Trish snapped a picture of the three of them.

"Rory and his godparents," Trish said.

Sammie was in too deep. It would be torture to love Jackson. He was part of her new family, her business partner, her friend and now the man she loved.

How stupid could she be?

She held Rory, gazing down at him and taking the comfort his sweet little wrinkled face could give her. She loved this teeny guy and focused on that love for now. "Hello, Rory. I'm your Aunt Sammie. So glad to meet you, little one. I think I'm going to spoil you just a little bit."

Jackson stroked his hand tenderly over Rory's head. "He'll have us both wrapped around his finger," he whispered to her.

Wonderful. She'd walk out of this room loving two Worth males and only the younger of them, if she was fortunate enough, would ever love her back.

* * *

Exactly one week later Sammie sat on Callie's sofa, holding little Rory in her arms. He was eight pounds of perfect, swaddled in powder-blue bunting. She glanced around the once masculine, custom-built rooms, seeing Callie's soft touches throughout and Rory's baby equipment everywhere. A bassinette was set up next to the fireplace, a baby swing sat in the far corner of the room and a diaper bag stood at the ready on the end table beside her.

"This really is baby central," Sammie said.

"It's a little overwhelming right now," Callie said, sipping herbal tea. She closed her eyes to the sensation. "But it goes with the territory."

"Yeah, it does. Babies need stuff."

Callie laughed.

She looked incredibly well after having delivered a baby last week. Already her shape was coming back. She'd be one of those women who in two months' time you'd never guess had ever been pregnant.

"Thanks, this tea you made me is yummy."

"It's my favorite, sweet and spicy."

Callie nodded. "Just like the two of us."

"You're the sweet one." Sammie gazed down at Rory and felt an uncanny closeness with him. He was beautiful in every way. She felt the same way about her friend.

"I can be spicy, too, you know."

"You're a mother now. You can't say things like that."

Callie giggled. "Tagg can't wait for me to be spicy again."

Sammie covered Rory's ears. "Callie."

She giggled once more, this time putting her hand to her deflated belly. "Oh, it hurts to laugh." Then she added. "But it feels good."

Sammie smiled. "I'm glad to be of use."

Callie sent her new little son a proud smile and her eyes misted up. "I can't believe he's mine."

Seeing the strong emotion on her friend's face put Sammie in a sentimental mood. "He's a perfect combination of you and Tagg. You made a miracle, Callie. It's truly amazing."

Callie glanced at her son, whose eyes had closed in sleep. "He is."

"I'm glad you found your happiness, Cal. You deserve it."

Her friend stared into her eyes with kindness and love. "You deserve it, too. You'll find your happiness. Soon."

"Soon?" Sammie began shaking her head and then stopped when a thought crossed her mind. "Well, I did get a call from a detective in Boston working on my case. They think they've located Allen, the embezzler. He set his stakes higher this time with a wealthy heiress and she caught on to him. She's apparently smarter than I was. I'm waiting to hear what happens next. The scum might just get his due. Maybe."

"Oh, I hope so."

Sammie still smarted from the betrayal of trust. She'd always have wounds, both financial and emotional, from Allen's deception. She only hoped he would get caught so he couldn't swindle any more women out of their innocence and money. "Putting Allen in jail would make me very happy."

"I think it's time for you to find another kind of happiness, Sammie," Callie said, her face suddenly becoming animated. "Tagg has an old friend coming over for the day next weekend. His name is Bryan McCormick. He has a beautiful piece of property north of Red Ridge. I'd love for you to meet him. You can have dinner with the three of us."

Sammie's shoulders stiffened. "Are you matchmaking?"

"Hell, yeah, I am. Can't you tell?"

"Thanks, Callie. But I can't."

Callie set her teacup down and stared into Sammie's eyes,

looking concerned. "Why can't you? Aren't you ready yet, honey? Are you still hurting from what Allen did to you?"

Sammie squirmed in her seat. Callie's worry only added to her culpability. She couldn't hold back the truth from her friend anymore. Not when Callie seemed so hopeful just seconds ago. She couldn't sit here, holding Callie's precious newborn son and lie to her friend any longer. She'd already had too many attacks of guilt. "Because…because I have feelings for someone else. Strong feelings."

Callie's eyes flickered. "Really?"

Sammie nodded.

And then Callie began doing mental calculations. Tapping her finger to her lips, she stared at Sammie and responded as if thinking out loud. "It's got to be either Sonny or Jackson, right? Or is that a silly question?"

Sammie glanced at the baby, unable to make eye contact with her friend. She answered quietly, "Silly question."

While Sammie felt like a fool for falling for a wealthy good-looking cowboy, a man who had women lining up for a chance at him, a man who was out of her league and wanted nothing to do with commitment, oddly Callie didn't flinch, shake her head or react in a negative way at all. "Okay. Tell me more."

Sammie lifted her gaze to hers. "Why did you think it was Sonny?"

"One day Jackson made a snarky remark about you running with Sonny in the mornings. I made a few assumptions based on the edge in his voice."

"Sonny's very nice."

"But Jackson is *very*…"

"Fill in the blank, Callie. Jackson is…*amazing*." She sounded like a girl with a teenage crush. But she wasn't. She'd gotten to know Jackson Worth pretty well, and despite all of her internal warnings she'd still fallen head over heels for him. That had to mean something.

Callie smiled. "You're in love."

Sammie tugged on a short lock of her hair. "It's ridiculous and so wrong."

"It's not ridiculous at all."

And for the next thirty minutes, Sammie told her everything, from waking up in Las Vegas with Jackson beside her to their secret pact, from Jackson's attempts to protect her during the dust storm to working together day and night and finally how she melted when she witnessed the love Jackson had for Rory. Sammie left out the most intimate details of their sexual encounters, but Callie was married to a Worth and could connect the dots easily. She knew all about the Worths' sex appeal.

"The thing I'm most sorry about is keeping this from you. I felt awful about it. I didn't want you to be disappointed in Jackson. It really wasn't his fault."

"You mean he can't help being irresistible to women?"

"That too, but really and truly the Vegas thing wasn't his fault. I was all over him."

"You drank too much."

"I should've known better. And we've managed to work together just fine after that. But then there was that awful dust storm and Jackson was so protective of me. He really was a gentleman the entire time. And I realized then that life is short. We could have died." Sammie shook her head. "Oh, I don't know, Callie. I was doing just fine...until I fell in love with him." She gave her friend the sorriest look she knew how to give, pleading with her. "Please don't be angry. I hope you forgive me for not telling you all this before. I feel so stupid."

Callie came over to sit beside her. She squeezed Sammie's shoulders gently, mindful not to wake Rory. "I'm not really angry. I get it. Remember how I acted with Tagg? I did the same thing with him that you did with Jackson because I thought I'd never have another chance. As for forgiving you, I do. I wish you'd have confided in me earlier, but I understand it's an awkward situation for both of you. I placed a lot of faith in Jackson to keep his hands off you and maybe I should have thought things through more."

"No, none of this is your fault, Callie. Please don't think that way. And don't be angry with Jackson either. Like I said, this is all on me."

"I should ring his neck," Callie said lightly before she smiled. "But I won't."

Sammie let out a sigh of relief and tears stung the back of her eyes. "Oh, Callie. Thank you for being so understanding. I'll be fine, really."

Callie touched the baby's cheek lovingly, her eyes filled with awe and delight. "This little guy puts everything in perspective for me," she said softly. "Not that I'd ever get mad at you for following your heart. So what's your plan of action?"

"M-my plan? I don't know what you mean?"

Callie narrowed her eyes. "Don't tell me you're going to step back and do nothing?"

"N-nothing? What do you think I should do?"

"Fight for Jackson."

Sammie blinked her eyes. She'd never expected to hear those words coming from Callie's lips. "But he's told me and the whole universe that he's not—"

"Neither was Tagg. Remember, he had a past, too. He'd been hurt. He never thought he'd fall in love again. Jackson's a good guy but he needs a jolt of reality. He needs you."

"No, no he doesn't."

Callie's voice deepened with determination. "You have to try, Sammie. If you don't, you'll never forgive yourself. You'll wonder all of your life if you'd missed something spectacular. Look at me. I'm living proof of it. If I hadn't been bold in that honky-tonk in Reno and gone after what I wanted, then I wouldn't be sitting here right now. I wouldn't be a Worth. And our little Rory would have been a fleeting notion of my wildest dreams."

Sammie glanced at Rory. He slept peacefully, wrapped up in the embrace of love from so many in this family. He was a miracle and Callie believed that Sammie could have the same type of life, a husband and a family. With Jackson.

"It's impossible, Callie," she said, fearful of hoping. "Jackson's ex is in town. Blair made a special point of coming to the grand opening the other day to announce that she was going after him. She wants him back."

"So?"

"So, maybe that's what he's wanted all along. She claims he's hers for the taking."

"That doesn't mean you have to hand him over, just like that. Trust me when I say Blair Caulfield isn't the right woman for him. I can't imagine how you'd feel seeing him with her and knowing you didn't give yourself a fighting chance."

Sammie's hope register began to climb. Callie seemed so sure, and Sammie was a different woman today than the one who'd let a man bamboozle her out of her life's earnings. She wasn't naïve anymore. This time she'd know exactly what she was getting into and what she'd stand to lose. Her eyes would be wide open when she put herself out there.

You can't win if you don't play, Sammie.

"I know you're right, Callie. I'll think of something."

Callie smiled, satisfied. "You won't be sorry."

Sammie would listen to her friend and her own heart. Jackson's love was definitely worth the risk.

Ten

For the seventh time this week, Jackson glanced at Trish's email on his phone. It was a candid photo taken on the day the baby was born, captioned The Godparents. "Sorry I didn't send this sooner," Trish had written, "the three of you look great."

The picture of Jackson, Sammie and Rory *did* look great. The expression of pure joy on Sammie's face was hard for Jackson to shake. He'd managed to glance at the picture at least once a day since the email had come through. And each time he looked at it, something warm and thrilling happened inside his gut. He welcomed the sensation and smiled at the photo before clicking it off.

He headed for the shower in his apartment, anticipating the hot steam soaking through to his bones and relaxing him. It had been a long, grueling day of meetings and appointments and his day wasn't over yet.

He had to keep his wits about him. He was due to pick

Blair up for a date in less than an hour. Jackson hadn't been able to put her off any longer. She'd been calling and showing up at his office unannounced. A part of him had been flattered, another part had been wary and now he was just ready to get it over with.

Jackson would have to play her game to get what he wanted.

He loosened his tie and lifted it over his head. Next he undid the buttons on his shirt and pulled his arms free of the sleeves just as the doorbell rang.

Throwing his arms back into his shirt, he shut off the shower and pulled out his wallet. "Coming," he called as he walked to the door. He expected to see his laundry service delivering his dry cleaning. But as he opened the door Blair stood there, wearing a glossy smile, her blond hair falling in waves over a beige coat lined with fur that ran all the way to the hem at her knees. A matching handbag hung from her shoulder and she held a grocery bag in her arms. "Hi."

She stepped past him, walking inside his apartment and taking in the entry and living space beyond. Then she whirled around to face him, focusing on his state of undress. "Nice."

"What are you doing here?" he asked, although he had more than a clue. The grocery bag and her early appearance were a dead giveaway.

"I'm making you dinner."

She took off her coat and his gaze immediately flew to her slinky dress. It looked like lingerie, the chocolate-brown and tan material leaving nothing to the imagination. Lace in strategic places allowed glimpses of her soft skin. Her plumped-up breasts overflowed the cups that were meant to hold her in. Jackson felt a tug at something vulnerable and weak inside him. "I was planning on taking you to dinner."

She grinned. "It'll be more fun this way, Jackson. I make

a wonderful beef dish I know you'll adore. Where's your kitchen?"

He pointed and then followed her. "Did you bring the deed?"

"We'll talk business after dinner. I brought this great French pinot noir. You'll love it." She entered the kitchen and put her grocery bag down. She pulled out a bottle and handed it to him. "Will you open the wine?"

Jackson went to his wine room just off the kitchen and came back with a corkscrew as she set out the ingredients for dinner on the smooth black granite countertop. She found two stemless crystal goblets as he unscrewed the cork and poured the wine.

She sidled up next to him, brushing his shoulder, and her scent surrounded him. He handed her a glass and she smiled as she lifted it toward his. "To new beginnings."

He held his glass steadily away from her. "First the deed, Blair."

The evening wouldn't progress further until he had first-hand evidence that she owned the property in question. She wasn't going to call all the shots.

"You are a stickler," she said with a coy pout designed to destroy a man's defenses. If Jackson didn't know better, it might have worked on him, too. As it was, he was taken by her beauty and couldn't find the words to toss her out of his penthouse apartment.

She rummaged through her handbag and came out with the deed. "Here you go. Take a look. It's authentic."

Jackson took a minute to read and reread the terms of the deed. It was authentic and the land had, in fact, been transferred to her from old man Weaver.

He sipped wine, staring into her blue eyes. "How'd you get him to sell, Blair?"

"Why is it so important to you?" she asked in a whisper.

"I've offered him twice what that land was worth every year for the past ten years. That's the only strip of land in a three-mile radius that doesn't belong to the Worths. The property needs protecting and should be left as is."

"I won't sell it off to those real estate developers if—"

"If what? I fall in love with you again? I can't promise that. We can't go back in time, Blair. We're both different people now."

"Would it be so bad to try?" she said softly, and he almost forgot about her blackmail. "I'm only asking for a chance, Jackson. We could start tonight."

Jackson remained silent, thinking as he eyed her over the wineglass. She was beautiful and sexy and everything Jackson had once thought he wanted in a woman.

Sammie's face popped into his mind then. The picture of the two of them holding little Rory was seared into his memory. The image was his lifeboat to cling to when he felt himself drowning. He held firm. "Tell me about Weaver."

Blair sighed wistfully and shot him a sad smile. "Pearson Weaver is my father. My mother had an affair with him the year before I was born. They were both married at the time. My mother wasn't known for her discretion, but she did keep that secret all of her life. When she took ill, she finally told me the truth. Pearson was so darn sorry about never acknowledging me, he didn't know what to do to make it up to me. I didn't ask for the land, but he gave it to me to prove that he cared about me all these years. It was the only thing of worth he really had. That, and my mother's love for a short time."

Jackson blinked. He'd never expected this, and the surprise must have registered on his face because Blair looked away in shame for a second.

Then she shrugged. "I think I always knew that Daniel Caulfield wasn't really my dad. Life wasn't grand in the

Caulfield household. My folks fought all the time and, occasionally, Daniel would look at me and question my mother's faithfulness. I hated every minute I spent in Red Ridge. I couldn't wait to leave town."

It wasn't an excuse for hurting him the way she did, but it was a reason he could possibly try to understand. "You never told me that."

"I was already the poor girl from the wrong side of the tracks to your family. Adding *illegitimate* to my list of flaws wouldn't have gone over too well."

Jackson took another sip of wine, trying to imagine what Blair must have gone through when she realized that her whole life had been a lie.

It wouldn't do to argue that his family had never looked unkindly upon Blair until she'd broken his heart. She'd betrayed him in the worst possible way. He wasn't ready to forgive her and needed time to let this all sink in. "Cook the meal, Blair. I need to take a shower."

She glanced at the ribbon of skin exposed by his unbuttoned shirt and lifted beckoning, beautiful eyes to his. Her expression left no doubt that she wanted an invitation to join him. Rejecting a gorgeous willing female wasn't easy under any circumstances, but turning his back on Blair took all of his willpower.

He swore an oath as he headed down the hallway, the image of Sammie and Rory nudging his brain once again—his lifeline pulling him to shore. He stripped off his clothes and stepped into the shower stall, hoping the soap and steam would help to cleanse away his perplexed thoughts. Maybe then he'd gain some clarity.

Sammie put the finishing touches on her makeup and stood back from the bathroom mirror to see her creation. The smoky look accentuated her brown eyes and made her entire appearance seem altogether different. She slashed bronzer across her cheeks, painted her lips with cherry-red lipstick and then air-kissed to the mirror. "Jackson Worth… you can't ignore me another night."

Ever since the grand opening and Rory's birth, Jackson had kept his distance. She knew he was a busy man and, after seeing that Boot Barrage had gotten off to a good start, he'd probably moved on to his next business venture. The shop was holding steady, acquiring new customers every day. Sammie was in her element when she was at the boutique.

She spent time with Callie and the baby whenever she could and Trish had recruited her to work at the General Store at Penny's Song in the afternoons when she was at the ranch. That's when Sammie had come up with the idea. She decided tonight she would kill two birds with one stone. She would pop over to Jackson's place and hope for the best.

Sammie spoke a silent vow not to allow self-doubt to deter her. To spur her confidence, she wore a new black knit dress that clung to her skin like a well-fitted glove. The dress zipped down from the valley between her breasts to the hem landing five inches above her knees. There wasn't much material to the dress but that wasn't her secret weapon.

That's where the Mariannas came in. The inky leather boots had piqued Jackson's interest the day of the grand opening and tonight Sammie was going all out. She sat down on the edge of her bed and slipped her feet with their blood-red painted toenails into the sandaled boots and laced them up to her knees. The heels gave her four extra inches and made her legs seem coltishly long.

Sammie avoided the mirror for fear she'd lose her nerve. But what woman could resist a glimpse at a transformation like that? After ten minutes of stalling she finally took a good look at herself in the mirror. The whole outfit screamed

"Do me," and Sammie was seconds away from tossing out the whole idea.

But Callie's words kept echoing in her ear. *Fight for Jackson. Fight for Jackson.*

And her friend was right. If she didn't try, she'd never know.

"It's time I see the inside of Jackson's penthouse," Sammie whispered. Then she picked up her purse, carefully placed the papers she'd drawn up inside and walked out of her apartment with newfound confidence.

On the drive to Jackson's penthouse, she sang along with country tunes on the radio, reminded herself to file her taxes and thought about a new chicken pesto recipe she was going to try. Otherwise she'd think too hard about what she was about to do. She was far from the vixen who'd stared back at her in the mirror minutes ago—keeping her mind busy was her best bet to ensure that she wouldn't lose her nerve.

It wasn't a far drive, just a ten-minute jaunt down major streets to get to the outskirts of Scottsdale. When she reached Jackson's stunning building with its terrace views of the surrounding hilltops, Sammie parked her car. Armed with her sketches, which admittedly she could've shown Jackson at the boutique, she got out, announced herself as Mr. Worth's guest to the doorman and was allowed entrance to the building. The ride up to the penthouse took only seconds, thanks to an express elevator. When the doors opened, she took a deep breath, steeled her nerves and walked to his door.

She knocked.

Only silence came from behind the door.

She knocked again, louder.

She heard footsteps and braced herself, plastering a smile on her face.

The door opened.

Blair Caulfield?

She looked Sammie up and down. Then her gaze landed on her Mariannas and recognition dawned. "Nice boots. You're Jackson's partner, right?"

Sammie's first thought was what the heck was Blair doing here. And her second thought was that at least the woman remembered she was Jackson's *partner* and not his employee.

Sammie struggled to keep her smile from fading. She hadn't expected this, but she couldn't say she was taken by complete surprise. The pungent scent of herbs and garlic penetrated her slightly numbed senses. She realized in that moment what Blair was doing here and a stabbing pain entered her heart. "Yes, I'm Sammie Gold."

"Blair," she stated. "We met the other day." She flicked her hair back and blocked the doorway as if she owned the place.

"I remember."

"How can I help you?"

Suddenly, Sammie took hold of her emotions. "I'm looking for Jackson."

"He's in the shower," Blair said, matter of factly.

Everything shut down inside and déjà vu set in. She felt the betrayal settle into her bones. It was a familiar feeling.

Your fiancé is a con artist, Ms. Gold. I'm afraid he's managed to embezzle all of your funds.

Jackson hadn't stolen her money. Quite the opposite, he'd helped her make her way financially, but he'd stolen something far worse. And the pain burned like wildfire through her system, ravaging her body in just seconds. She had no claim on Jackson and he'd never once alluded to wanting a relationship with her. But the sting of betrayal was sharp regardless.

They'd had sex, period. And silly her, she thought that maybe after a friendship developed and Jackson had gotten to know her, she might have a chance with him.

Boy, had she been wrong.

"Oh. Well…I just came to give him these papers." She refused to fumble. Elegantly, as if she were a queen, she lifted the manila file out of her handbag.

Just as she was about to lay the papers on Blair and leave Jackson's voice stopped her. "Blair, is someone at the door?"

Sammie froze, and time seemed to click into slow motion.

His voice grew louder as he approached. "Is it my dry cleaning?"

"No, it's just me," she said, her voice squeakier than she would have liked. "Sammie."

Jackson appeared in the entry, hastily throwing his arms into his shirt. In his hand, he held a wallet. His wheat-blond hair was dark with moisture and combed away from his face. Of course he looked gorgeous. "Sammie?"

"She came over to drop off some papers," Blair said to him.

Jackson took one look at Sammie, raking his gaze from top to bottom. His eyes lingered on her boots. The Mariannas had the effect she'd hoped for. Except right now she only wanted out of this awkward situation. "Here you go," she said regally, handing over the papers. "It's an idea I had for Penny's Song. It's all in writing and nothing that can't wait."

She glanced at Blair, who wore a satisfied expression, much like a cat who'd slurped a pint of milk.

Jackson darted glances at the two of them and began shaking his head. "This isn't what it looks like, Sammie."

Blair's mouth dropped open in surprise and then with one hand on her voluptuous hip, her lips twitched. "It's exactly what it looks like."

"Be quiet, Blair," he said, keeping his gaze fastened on Sammie.

She stared at the droplets of water dotting his strong chest. "You don't have to explain," Sammie said, but she couldn't keep accusation from her tone. "It's okay. I'm just on my way out. I have…I have a date."

Jackson's brows flew up. "Dressed like that?"

Sammie blinked. Was that a compliment or a put down? She didn't want to take the time to find out. "Uh…huh."

It wasn't really a lie. She did tell Sonny she'd meet him for coffee one night this week. And it looked like tonight was the night.

Jackson's voice held conviction as he looked sharply at her. "You're not going out with Sonny looking like that."

Sammie held in her anger, feigning a noncommittal attitude. She responded sweetly, "I don't think it's any of your business who I go out with or how I dress. Don't worry about the papers right now. I'm late. I have to go."

She pivoted, walked out and almost made it to the elevator before Jackson reached for her, gripping her around the waist. His touch made her ache inside and it was the hardest thing for her not to turn around and fall into his arms. But Jackson didn't let that stop him. He drew her up close from behind and spoke softly, his breath whispering over her ear. "You didn't come here dressed like that to drop off papers, Sammie."

Sammie's chest rose in a deep, sad sigh. Her heart was breaking into a thousand pieces—it was agony not to admit the truth to Jackson. But Sammie couldn't let another man make a fool out of her. She had to walk away with her dignity this time. She'd learned at least that much from Allen's deception. She stepped out of his grasp and walked into the elevator. Only right before the doors closed did she turn to look into his troubled blue eyes.

"Blair is waiting for you."

Jackson watched the elevator doors close. Sammie's hurt expression, no matter how hard she'd tried to conceal it, ripped him apart. He jammed his hand into his wet hair, narrowed his eyes and swore a dozen oaths before whirling around and heading back to the penthouse.

It looked bad. He couldn't deny it. Blair had answered his door with a proprietary air, while he'd been steps behind, coming to greet Sammie half dressed. She'd made natural assumptions about where the night was heading and, in truth, up until now, he hadn't been sure that her assumptions would have proved wrong.

"She's a wiry little thing, isn't she?" Blair said, waiting for him by the threshold.

Jackson strode past her, grabbed the file Sammie left for him, and headed to the terrace. He shoved the sliding doors open and stepped outside. He stood there staring out for long moments, not really seeing the peaceful hillsides to the west or the quiet street below. All he saw was the devastation on Sammie's face as the elevator doors closed.

He'd played with fire in Sammie Gold and she'd gotten burned.

The hell of it was, he wanted to stop her and demand she not go out with Sonny. Jackson studied his feelings. He didn't want her for himself, not in the long run, but he didn't want any other man to claim her either—especially not his friend.

She'd been vulnerable, hurt and picking up the pieces of her life when she settled in Arizona, hoping for a fresh start. Jackson winced, squeezing his eyes closed for a second thinking about how he'd only managed to injure her more. Her crestfallen face in that elevator flashed into his mind again. He'd seen something else in that moment—Sammie's look of utter disgust, as if he was the scum of the earth.

A little voice inside his head whispered, "She's a grown woman. She knew what she was getting herself into."

But Jackson shook off that thought. He wouldn't transfer blame to her. He'd done everything wrong with Sammie Gold.

Under the dim light of the terrace lantern, he opened the folder and flipped through the pages Sammie had brought over. They were sketches of custom-made children's cowboy boots with a Penny's Song logo of her own design stamped into leather. The boots were to be a parting gift for the children who'd come through the facility on their road to recovery. And it was to be her contribution to the family charity. She had notes written on the sketches. *Is this a silly idea? Do you think the children would like these? Black leather for boys? Tan for girls?*

Jackson stared at the sketches. Minutes ticked by.

"Dinner is getting cold," Blair said from behind him.

Jackson didn't want to look at her. He didn't want to see what his life had become because of the injury Blair Caulfield had inflicted on him. He couldn't trust her. Not now, not even after her admission about why she'd hated Red Ridge so much. Why she felt the need to run off.

The contrast of the two women in his life was stark and far-reaching. Whereas Blair had destroyed his faith in many ways and made him shun commitment by her betrayal, resorting now to what he'd classify as emotional blackmail to get what she wanted, Sammie had been strong, determined, generous. She'd made him laugh and made him lust and fit into his family perfectly. *She* had never asked anything of him. *She* would never resort to blackmail or anything dishonest to get what she wanted.

"Jackson?" Blair stepped onto the terrace to face him. Something she saw in his gaze had her stammering. "D-did you hear me?"

"I don't want dinner."

"But it's ready and wait—"

He walked into the kitchen and she followed. Once there,

he picked up the handbag sitting on the counter and handed it to her. "I think you should leave, Blair."

Indignation raged in her eyes. "You're kicking me out?"

"I'm asking you to leave." He'd been raised to show a lady good manners.

"You don't want to do this."

"Yes, I do."

With a hand to her back, he guided her toward the front door. She went reluctantly. "There's nothing between us but old memories better off forgotten."

As they reached the entrance to his penthouse, she swung around to meet his gaze. Gone now was her confident attitude that had men begging for her attention. She looked defeated and exposed. On her it actually looked better, more real and much less calculated.

She swallowed and gave him her last pitch. "What about the land deal? You're willing to give that up *for her?*"

Jackson blinked and then studied her face, letting her comment sink all the way in. Blair had hit the nail on the head and suddenly Jackson had the clarity he'd been seeking. "Yeah, I think I am. Do what you will with Weaver's land, Blair. I'm not for sale."

Her face flamed and she sent him a glare. He only smiled at her in return. In a way he felt sorry for her. And she sensed her ultimate defeat in his smile. Her shoulders slumped and she nodded. Nothing good came from kicking a dead horse. Blair understood that and, for a moment, Jackson saw the sweet, lovely Blair Caulfield of his youth.

"I knew you were in love with her," she said, "the second I saw the two of you together."

"Well, then you're more astute than I am, honey. Because I just figured that out about thirty seconds ago."

Eleven

Callie Sullivan Worth was Sammie's best friend and because of that, Jackson's sister-in-law refused to give him any answers. Sometimes he hated the strong bond of friendship that women shared. It was especially annoying now. Callie kept her lips sealed and wouldn't tell him what was going on with Sammie.

"She's out of town and will be back in a few days," Callie repeated. "That's all I'm allowed to tell you."

Jackson took a swig of beer. He couldn't very well argue with Callie. She was recovering from her delivery and not getting much sleep. The baby suckled underneath some clip-on material contraption to save her modesty. He heard the slurping sounds and if he wasn't so damn frustrated, he'd have walked out of the parlor and let her nurse the baby privately.

"She sure left in a quick hurry," he said, probing. Jackson had waited until the morning after their encounter at his apartment to seek Sammie out. Not going after her immediately had been a big mistake. How was he to know she'd leave town abruptly?

After he'd unceremoniously kicked Blair out of his apartment, he'd had to face his feelings for Sammie. And for the first time in his adult life, he'd been honestly scared. Emotions he'd tucked safely away had surfaced with a painful jab. The assault was a strange and wonderful combination of liberation. Up until the day he'd met her in Las Vegas, he'd been immunized against falling for a female again, but getting to know Sammie had changed all the rules. He wasn't immune any longer. No, now he was vulnerable and the affliction was love.

He'd gone to her apartment this morning and knocked until he'd roused her next-door neighbors. They'd opened their door and given him disgruntled looks, grumbling. He hadn't been able to reach her by phone either. But she had granted him one brief text message that read:

Something came up. Will be gone for a few days. Boot Barrage is covered.

Like he gave a damn if the boutique was staffed well enough in her absence.

"I can't say anymore." Callie was adamant and there was no changing her mind.

"I told you everything," he said, taking a bigger swig of beer. "I came clean and admitted my mistakes. I don't want to make any more of them."

Callie smiled. "You won't. I have faith in you. You'll do the right thing."

Tagg entered the room, took one look at the exasperation on Jackson's face and grinned. "Welcome to the club."

"Hey," Callie said with phony indignation. "I'm sitting right here."

Tagg bent to kiss her cheek and then sat down next to her. "I know. And I'm glad of it. That's all I meant."

She angled him a dubious look. "Smooth talker."

"That's me." Then he turned to Jackson. "So how bad is it?"

"Hell. I don't know. Sammie left town. I have a feeling I'm not her favorite person right now."

"An understatement," Tagg said.

"Not helping," Callie said.

"So what now?" Jackson bypassed Tagg to ask the question of Callie.

"As soon as you get the chance, tell her how you feel," his sister-in-law said.

"New territory for you, isn't it?" Tagg *wasn't* helping.

"Yeah, it is. So, you think she'll forgive me?"

Callie shook her head slowly and he could see in her eyes how hard it was to keep her promise to her friend. Her voice lent sympathy. "I can't discuss her with you, Jackson. I'm sorry. But I can give you my opinion. She didn't say I couldn't do that."

"Which is?"

"Really think about what you want before you approach her. Because she's at a breaking point and—"

"I'd hog-tie you and drag you through town if you do damage to that girl again," Tagg interjected.

Callie agreed. "I'd take up the reins with Freedom and do it myself," she said to him.

Jackson drew a steady breath. "Trust me. That's not going to happen. I…love her."

Both Tagg and Callie stared at him. Both blinked simultaneously. It was sort of strange how in tune they were with each other. They were soul mates. And he kinda figured Sammie was his soul mate. The notion snuck up on him, but the more he thought about it, the more he liked the idea.

Callie spoke in a quietly awed voice. "I'm thrilled about that, Jackson."

He nodded, feeling less confident about a woman than he had at any other time in his adult life. A recollection of Sammie's expression when those elevator doors closed flashed in his mind. "There's a lot at risk. I may need your help."

"As long as it doesn't breach my promise to Sammie, I'll do what I can."

"Thanks," he said before tipping his beer bottle and finishing it off.

"Rory needs to be burped. Which one of you two cowboys is up for the task?" And like a magician's sleight of hand, Callie produced a satisfied little Rory from underneath the breastfeeding garment.

Jackson offered instantly. "Hand him over. I'm still working on being his favorite uncle."

"Yeah, he might cheer you up," Tagg said, carefully transferring the baby over. "You look like hell. Uh," he said, darting a glance at Callie. "*Heck.* You look like heck."

"I can always count on you to tell me straight, little brother."

The next two days dragged and Jackson was getting antsy. He'd checked in with the staff at Boot Barrage, showing up there twice each day hoping to hear news about Sammie, but the girls didn't know much except to say that Sammie called them once in the morning and once at the end of the day to answer any questions they had. All in all, the staff seemed to be holding their own in Sammie's absence.

On the third day, as he drove past Boot Barrage, he noticed Sammie's car in the parking lot behind the boutique. It was early, and the store wasn't due to open for half an hour.

Finally he'd get Sammie alone.

He parked his car next to hers and used his key to enter

through the back entrance. When he walked inside, he found
her sitting at her desk, going over paperwork.

He had to smile at the vision she made. Beautiful in her
unique way, wearing a gray soft jersey dress that draped in
folds across her chest, a pale pink belt around her waist and
matching midcalf boots of the same color. Jackson drank
in the sight of her.

She glanced up from the work on her desk and gave him
a casual smile. "Hi, Jackson."

His heart filled with dread. Something was up with her.
She wasn't angry, hurt or upset. Instead, she seemed calm
and indifferent. She'd smiled. Not a good sign.

"Sammie. We need to talk."

"I agree," she said, rising from her desk and approaching.
The scent of her sweet citrus perfume flared in his nostrils.
This was his Sammie. "There's something I have to tell you.
I think you're going to like it."

Her assurance and composed demeanor made him think
just the opposite. He wasn't going to like anything she had
to say. There was a wall of indifference on her face and a
new flash of determination in her eyes.

"You don't have to be my partner anymore."

The sight of Jackson stirred everything female inside
her. Loving him was difficult, but finding a way not to love
him would be even harder. Still, Sammie was determined
to move through this rough patch and get on with her life.
She had to be strong. And brave. She wasn't willing to give
up Callie's friendship or the Worth family's for that matter.
They were her family now, so she'd convinced herself that
this was a start, a good way to break some of her ties with
Jackson—the man she loved from deep down in her heart.

"Sammie," he said coming to stand directly in front of
her. He wore a tan felt hat today, a pair of faded jeans and a

chambray shirt, hardly attire for a day of business at the office. He had stubble on his face and his eyes were rimmed with fatigue. "Just listen to me. I never meant to hurt you. I swear it. What you saw the other night wasn't what it looked like. And I know it looked pretty doggone bad."

She halted him with her hand. "Stop. You don't have to explain anything to me. I'm not your girlfriend. You weren't cheating on me. You had every right to see Blair Caulfield. To do whatever you did with her at your apartment."

"Nothing. I did nothing except throw her out."

Sammie's resolve began to melt. "You threw her out?"

"Yes, I did. After you showed up, I realized I'd made a mistake. She was holding something over my head that I thought I wanted very badly."

"Her love?"

"No, Sammie. Not her love. She had land in her possession that I've been after for years. That land is a thin strip of property that should belong to the Worths. It was bartered away half a century ago and she knew I wanted it back. It was emotional blackmail. She'd give up her land, if I...if we—"

"I see." Sammie did see. This revelation was only more proof, more fuel to add to the fire that Jackson Worth would never be hers. Women went to great lengths to garner his attention and gain his love. No matter his confession, which was something at least, Sammie understood now that Jackson Worth wasn't the man for her.

But oh, how she loved him.

"Well, that's all fine and good, Jackson. Really."

His eyes narrowed and he sent her a doubtful look. "You forgive me?"

She shrugged and pretended nonchalance. "There's nothing to forgive. But if it makes you feel better, yes. I forgive you."

Jackson drew a deep breath and exhaled slowly, his nostrils flaring. "What's up with you today?"

Sammie launched into her good news. News that would break one tie to Jackson and free her from her prison of pain. "My ex was caught red-handed and green-backed."

"What?" Jackson's frustration clearly showed on his face.

"Allen was arrested. The police have confiscated all of his funds. Get this, they found him carrying thirty-thousand dollars on his person. Can you believe that? And they found hoards of cash at his residence, too. When I got the call, I flew to Boston to speak with the detectives. I'm happy to say, I'm no longer penniless. I'm getting most of my money back."

Going back to Boston provided her some time and space to see how futile loving Jackson was. It gave her a better perspective on her life and where it was heading. At the same time she realized she wasn't the only naive woman who'd been conned. Allen had left a string of innocent woman in his wake, cleaning them out of their savings and moving on. Sammie had been one of many. Misery loves company, they say. But Sammie didn't feel that way. She felt sorry for every one of those women who'd been bamboozled like she had been.

"That's great, Sammie." Jackson's face lit and he gave her a killer smile that was genuine and sincere.

Sammie couldn't look into that beaming megawatt smile and not be affected. But she forged on, refusing to be unintentionally conned by the hunky cowboy. Fool me once, shame on you. Fool me twice, shame on me. She couldn't let Jackson know how sad she was inside. How her hope had died. She couldn't show him her real feelings.

"It is. So you see, you don't need to explain anything to me. I didn't leave because I was upset with you. I had pressing business in Boston. And I'm back now. You have nothing to feel guilty about."

"I'm glad you're back, darlin'. I missed you."

Don't say things like that...pleeeeeze. "Well, thank you. And I'm glad you're here because now we can talk business."

Jackson's mouth pulled down. "Sammie, I'm not here to talk business."

"But I am, and since you're here, let me make you a proposition. I want to buy back your half of Boot Barrage...with interest, of course. You really didn't want to go into the shoe business with me. You did it as a favor to Callie. Which, by the way I greatly appreciate. But now you're off the hook. I'm in a position to buy you out. And that's what I'd like to do. You don't have to be my partner anymore."

Sammie said her spiel in a rush, wanting so badly to get the words out, to make Jackson see she meant business and was serious before he could stop her. Before her hard-won resolve would weaken. Every minute she spent with him did that...weakened her. And she couldn't let that happen. "Well, what do you think?"

Jackson studied her for a long time, his eyes raking over her and his breaths coming in rapid, short bursts. If he was angry, cool Jackson Worth would never let on. He never gave away his feelings. He'd built his defenses up for so long she doubted he'd ever learn to shed them even for the right person.

"Well?" she pressed him.

He took another few seconds, contemplating. "I'll have to think on it."

Before she could argue her point further, Jackson stepped closer and reached out to skim his hand along her arm. She froze from his touch and steeled herself against the impact of it. Too many good memories emerged from that one single slight caress. The laughter they shared; the love of family; the hot, hungry lovemaking.

She gazed into his eyes, seeing in them something dangerously sweet and understanding. Had he seen through her ploy? Did he know her pride was injured and she was scrambling to keep her dignity? Did he guess she was a fraud, lying to protect herself from future heartache? Or had he been just as taken by the touch of their skin?

"I'll let you know soon, sweetheart."

He turned and walked away. When she heard the back door slam shut, Sammie jumped, shaken by his appearance here and by the tremors racking her body. "That went well," she whispered, broken and alone. She lowered her head into her hands and closed her eyes.

She could grant herself ten minutes of self-pity before Boot Barrage opened.

Then she'd have to put up a good front for the boot-buying world to see.

Callie was a saint for listening to Sammie's moans and groans this past week. She'd cried on the phone with her, and Callie had comforted her in every way she knew how. Callie never once reprimanded her or told her she was an ingrate for not seeing her good fortune. Her ex was getting his just due, charged on ten counts of embezzlement and fraud, and she'd been assured he'd serve prison time. She was getting most of her money back. Boot Barrage was thriving now.

Sammie had work she loved and good friends. She had just about everything a girl could want. Yet Jackson hadn't given her his answer yet. She hadn't seen or heard from him since the morning he'd shown up at Boot Barrage. That should be a good thing. She should get used to not seeing him all the time, yet she missed him like crazy.

Sammie turned on the car radio as she drove to Red

Ridge. She punched the button for a rock station and the boisterous music blocked out her thoughts. She had to stop feeling sorry for herself. She had to forget about Jackson. Callie's invitation for a picnic at the lake, with Trish, Meggie and Rory, was just the outlet she needed to take her mind off of Jackson. She'd packed a lunch and was happy to have this pleasant diversion on her day off.

When she pulled up to the designated area, she spotted Callie near the lake bank and waved. She parked her car along a grassy rim twenty feet away and loaded down her arms with a basket, blanket and presents for both of the children. She was looking forward to some baby love to make her feel better.

As she approached, she noted Callie's smile fade a little.

"Hi," Sammie said, putting down the items she held to give Callie a big hug. "It's good to see you."

"It's good to see you too." Callie spoke with an unsteady voice.

"Where's Rory?" Sammie noticed that Callie was the only one at the lake. "And Trish and Meggie?"

"They're not coming."

"Why not?"

"Because we're really not having a picnic today."

Sammie's face fell. She was so looking forward to it. "What's going on, Cal? Is the baby sick? Gosh, I hope not."

"No. That's not it, Sammie. Rory is fine. It's…it's…" She darted a glance toward a thicket of trees.

Suspicious now, Sammie questioned her friend with one word. "Callie?"

Callie's voice lowered to a breathy whisper. "I'm sorry for lying to you. I really am. I hope you will forgive me. I've got to go." Callie began walking up the grassy knoll.

"Go?" Confused and a little panicky, she called out. "Where are you going?"

Callie was halfway to her car before Sammie saw someone approaching from behind a tree.

Jackson.

Then it hit her. She'd been set up. "Callie Worth, you come back here right now."

Callie turned around and mouthed "Sorry" before she bounded into her car and drove off.

Sammie was left standing there, defenseless against Jackson's approach. He was dressed in a Western suit and string tie with the ends of his wheat-colored hair flipping against his collar. His outfit was in direct contrast to her baggy cargo pants and dingy pink T-shirt. Her hair was combed back tomboy style, held with a barrette. In short, she looked like hell and he looked good enough to devour whole.

"What are you doing here?" she asked in a gravelly, unhappy voice.

"I'm here for you."

"That's obvious. Callie just abandoned me." She gazed at the dust Callie's car had kicked up as she drove off.

"I came to tell you I've made my decision. I don't want to be your partner," he said.

"Okey dokey. That's fine. Thank you."

"I'll have the necessary papers drawn up."

Jackson was always on top of his game. "Fine." Her pulse pounded. She didn't like being alone with Jackson. He made her want things she wasn't ever going to get. "Is that all?"

"No, there's more," he said, cool as a cucumber.

He was smiling and that set her nerves to jingling. "What else?"

"You know where we are, don't you?"

Sammie rolled her eyes. "Yes, we're at the lake."

"Elizabeth Lake."

"Yes, Elizabeth Lake. So?"

"Just thought I'd mention that to you."

"Okay, so we've established that we're at Elizabeth Lake."

"And you know the legend of Elizabeth Lake, don't you?"

Sammie's face wrinkled as the notion struck. "Yes, it's where…it's where…uh, your great-great-grandfather saved your great-great-grandmother from drowning." Sammie knew of the other legend. The entire town of Red Ridge knew about it, from what she'd been told, but she refused to let her mind go there.

"Yes, that's how they first met. But just as important, it's also where every Worth man has ever proposed to his woman."

His woman? Sammie took a step back and began shaking her head. "So?"

Jackson moved in on her. "So, you love me."

Sammie's mouth opened. And then shut. She edged back some more.

"You love me, Sammie. Admit it."

"I'd be a fool to love you, Jackson. You're a confirmed bachelor." She felt herself slipping down the slope. With the lake directly behind her, she didn't have far to go before she reached the bank.

He kept smiling and moving closer. "Why else?"

"Well, I, uh…you're too darn good-looking for your own good."

"Thanks. Why else?"

She had less than a yard to go before she'd be wading in water. "You don't even have a clue how charming you are, which makes women want to give you anything you ask for."

"Really? I didn't know that."

"That's part of your appeal."

Jackson stared at her lips. "We're getting sidetracked here. You love me, remember?"

"I never said that." She leaned back, away from him. He was scaring her, giving her dashed hopes new life.

"So, you don't love me?" He actually looked injured.

Sammie inched back another foot and the heel of her boot touched water. "Why do you want to know?"

"Because a man kinda wants to know that the woman he loves, loves him back."

Sammie flinched and she almost lost her balance. Gorgeous Jackson Worth reached out to draw her to his chest. Her head tilted upward. She had no choice but to meet his eyes. "You *love* me?"

"I'm crazy about you, Sammie. And I'd like it if you didn't fall into the water before I proposed to you."

"Proposed?" Sammie's heart hammered. She was about to swoon, like a lady in waiting, but she held on. "Proposed what exactly?"

Jackson grinned, showing the twin notches grooved into his cheeks. He was beautiful when he smiled, dimples and all. "Sammie," he said, "haven't you been listening?"

"Well, actually…I uh, can't believe my own ears."

"Believe this," he said, gently lifting her up and twirling her around so that they traded places. She got her footing on solid earth, though her knees were ready to buckle. "I love you, Sammie Gold."

Jackson's midnight-blue eyes gleamed with the same intense emotion he'd reserved for Rory and Meggie. The brilliance of his gaze nearly knocked her out.

He kept talking, but Sammie only heard those three small words she'd never thought she'd hear coming from Jackson.

"…and I thought it was just the boots. I mean honestly, honey, no one wears boots the way you do. I don't usually get jealous and there I was ready to knock Sonny Estes into the next century when I thought—"

"You were jealous?"

He nodded. "Green with it."

Sammie smiled.

"Don't look so happy about it." His brows gathered as he frowned. "When we first met we made that stupid pact and it killed me not to touch you again. I wanted to so many times. And I told myself it was good you didn't remember that night too clearly, darlin'. Because that night in Vegas was hot and wild and I would've gladly offered you a repeat of the time you didn't remember."

Sammie's face flamed. This was all so surreal. She was standing with Jackson Worth and *he* was telling *her* how hot she was and how much he wanted her. It was a table-turner for sure.

"As it was, we got caught in the dust storm," he went on. "I was panicked that something would happen to you, Sammie. I think I loved you then and didn't realize it."

"You were wonderful that night, Jackson. You saved my life. You just keep saving me. How could I not love you?"

His face lit like a young boy and a deep smile spread across his face. "You said it. You love me."

She giggled. "I did say it. I do love you, Jackson. I love you very much. But I never thought you'd love me back. In fact, I tried talking myself out of loving you. I tried to convince myself you're not the man for me. And when I walked in on you and Blair, my world just sort of caved in around me."

"I swear to you, nothing happened with Blair."

"I believe you, Jackson. Maybe I didn't at the time. My vision sort of gets blurry when I see you with a blonde bomb-shell you once loved beyond distraction."

"Maybe I was just a kid too young to know my own heart, infatuated with a pretty girl," he said. "When Blair came back to town, I wasn't sure how I felt about her. But she knew what she wanted and wasn't above trying to ma-nipulate me to get it. I finally realized that I didn't want any part of her, her offer or that land if it meant losing you.

If I hurt you, I'm truly sorry. You are the last person in the world I'd ever want to hurt."

Sammie smiled and said softly, "You're doing a good job making up for it. Keep talking."

He chuckled, and the sound of his laughter eased the pain that had dwelled in her heart this past week.

"Blair and I were never right for each other. And I figured that out finally the other night when you showed up at my door. It all became clear to me and I have to thank you for giving me the closure with Blair I needed. No other woman I've ever met compares to you, Sammie. You're my present and my future and the only one I want in my life. If you'll have me."

Sammie's throat constricted. She couldn't believe her ears a second ago and now she couldn't believe her eyes. Jackson Worth got down on one knee. Magically, a diamond ring appeared in her line of vision…a stunner that sparkled under the Arizona sun and stole all of her breath.

"Sammie Gold, I love you with my whole heart. You make everything brighter in my life. I'm asking you to marry me and be my wife and if you do me the honor, I promise to be a good husband to you and love you forever. If you say yes, I also promise I won't dunk you into this lake so I can dive in to save you."

Sammie giggled again. "Yes, I'll marry you, Jackson. Because I love you so very much and because I don't need a dunking to know how much I want to be your wife."

Jackson rose then, satisfied. His gaze fastened on hers and all joking was put aside. With reverence he took her hand in his and placed the ring on her finger. As she slid it in place, both of them admired the way the diamond caught the light. It felt good on her hand. And right.

It was a perfect fit.

Jackson brought his lips to her fingers and kissed her softly with tenderness in his eyes. "I love you."

The next kiss joined their lips in a lovely, I'm-in-it-for-the-long-haul kind of kiss that said there would be plenty more where that came from so there was no need to rush.

As Jackson held her hand, they turned toward Elizabeth Lake. The sky was blue and the air was clear and gleaming water rippled and lapped at the shore where they stood. Sammie was a member of a very exclusive club of Worth women now. She would see her love blossom and grow beside a man of considerable honor and integrity.

Loving Jackson was a very good thing, Sammie decided.

And definitely worth the risk.

Two months later...

The Red Ridge Mountains loomed large and glorious against the horizon; horses whinnied and crimson dust spiraled up as the cars pulled to a stop on the site of the original Worth home. Tears of joy and humbling awe filled Sammie's eyes for the second time today. Emotions she couldn't tamp down swamped her as Jackson, her new husband, led her by the hand into Tagg and Callie's parlor after little Rory's baptism.

"I'm so honored to be Rory's godmother," she said, taking a seat on the sofa. Her eyes continued to mist, blurring her vision a little. She held gifts in her hands for everyone.

"Aw, Sammie." Jackson thumbed her tears dry, giving her the sweetest look. "I'm still Rory's favorite but you don't have to cry about it, sweetheart."

She laughed despite her nonsensical tears. In a few minutes the Worth family would know exactly why she was crying. "You won't be once he gets a load of these."

Sammie couldn't wait another second. The secret she'd

held on to for weeks was ready to spill out. She handed Callie a box with powder-blue wrapping. "This is for our godson."

Her friend accepted the gift. "This is so sweet of you. Thank you."

And then Sammie handed Trish a box decorated with pink and white flowers. "This is for baby Meggie."

"Thank you," Trish said graciously, showing the box to the baby on her lap. Immediately chubby hands reached for the pink ribbon.

"Please open them," Sammie urged.

Both women untied the ribbon, took off the wrapping paper and lifted the lids.

Callie found custom-made chocolate brown boots small enough to fit Rory's little feet in about a year, designed with tiny silver studs forming the letter W. "Oh, you didn't." Callie grinned as she showed off the boots.

"He'll learn to walk in boots," Sammie said and everyone, including Jackson, laughed.

Trish brought out Meggie's pair, designed in the same fashion with a silver-studded W and in exactly the same size, but these boots were candy-apple red. "I love these," Trish said.

Clay sized the boots to Meggie's feet. "Six more months and she'll be sashaying around in these."

"That's the plan," Sammie said. Then she glanced at the one box she had remaining wrapped with pink and blue tissue and tied with a white bow. Her heart overflowed with love when she set the last box on Jackson's lap.

"And this is for you," Sammie said, her eyes misting again.

Jackson stared down at the box. The other two women in the room gave a sharp gasp. The brothers were slower on the uptake, but Jackson simply appeared puzzled. "For me?"

She nodded. Quietly, she added, "For both of us."

Jackson's brows nudged his forehead. He took a big swallow and his hands shook as he removed the wrapping and opened the box. He stared down at teeny white boots, marked with the same "W" emblem and in the same size as all the others. His shock immediately transformed to an adoring look of love aimed toward her. "Are you saying…?"

"I'm saying our son or daughter will walk proud, too." She laid a hand over her abdomen and smiled. "But it will be a little while before our baby will fit into these boots."

Jackson set his strong hand carefully on her belly. His feelings showed in the beaming glow of his eyes and the absolute awe in his voice. "Our baby."

Then he grinned, a dimpled stadium-light bright smile that calmed all of her nerves and brought her great relief and joy.

"Yes, our baby."

Jackson rose from his seat and gently, tenderly lifted her up, blocking out the cheers and congratulations from his family members to kiss Sammie sweetly on the lips. Holding her tight, his fingers splayed into the short caramel strands of her hair, he whispered, "I wouldn't have figured boots to have changed my life so darn much for the better."

Sammie smiled and whispered back, "Never doubt the power of the boot."

"I never will again, Sweet Sammie. I promise you that."

And Sammie took that promise to heart along with his love and commitment. She still had a honeymoon to look forward to.

Jackson was taking her to Paris.

Las Vegas.

* * * * *

REQUEST YOUR FREE BOOKS!

2 FREE NOVELS PLUS 2 FREE GIFTS!

♥ Harlequin® *Desire*

ALWAYS POWERFUL, PASSIONATE AND PROVOCATIVE

YES! Please send me 2 FREE Harlequin Desire® novels and my 2 FREE gifts (gifts are worth about $10). After receiving them, if I don't wish to receive any more books, I can return the shipping statement marked "cancel." If I don't cancel, I will receive 6 brand-new novels every month and be billed just $4.30 per book in the U.S. or $4.99 per book in Canada. That's a saving of at least 14% off the cover price! It's quite a bargain! Shipping and handling is just 50¢ per book in the U.S. and 75¢ per book in Canada.* I understand that accepting the 2 free books and gifts places me under no obligation to buy anything. I can always return a shipment and cancel at any time. Even if I never buy another book, the two free books and gifts are mine to keep forever.

225/326 HDN FEF3

Name	(PLEASE PRINT)	
Address		Apt. #
City	State/Prov.	Zip/Postal Code

Signature (if under 18, a parent or guardian must sign)

Mail to the **Reader Service:**

IN U.S.A.: P.O. Box 1867, Buffalo, NY 14240-1867
IN CANADA: P.O. Box 609, Fort Erie, Ontario L2A 5X3

Not valid for current subscribers to Harlequin Desire books.

Want to try two free books from another line?
Call 1-800-873-8635 or visit www.ReaderService.com.

* Terms and prices subject to change without notice. Prices do not include applicable taxes. Sales tax applicable in N.Y. Canadian residents will be charged applicable taxes. Offer not valid in Quebec. This offer is limited to one order per household. All orders subject to credit approval. Credit or debit balances in a customer's account(s) may be offset by any other outstanding balance owed by or to the customer. Please allow 4 to 6 weeks for delivery. Offer available while quantities last.

Your Privacy—The Reader Service is committed to protecting your privacy. Our Privacy Policy is available online at www.ReaderService.com or upon request from the Reader Service.

We make a portion of our mailing list available to reputable third parties that offer products we believe may interest you. If you prefer that we not exchange your name with third parties, or if you wish to clarify or modify your communication preferences, please visit us at www.ReaderService.com/consumerschoice or write to us at Reader Service Preference Service, P.O. Box 9062, Buffalo, NY 14269. Include your complete name and address.

HDES11B

*Bestselling Harlequin® Blaze™ author Rhonda Nelson
is back with yet another irresistible Man out of Uniform.
Meet Jebb Willington—former ranger, current security
agent and all-around good guy. His assignment—to catch
a thief at an upscale retirement residence. The problem—
he's falling for sexy massage therapist Sophie O'Brien,
the woman he's trying to put behind bars....*

*Read on for a sneak peek at
THE PROFESSIONAL*

Available November 2012 only from Harlequin Blaze.

Oh, hell.

Former ranger Jeb Willingham didn't need extensive army training to recognize the telltale sound that emerged roughly ten feet behind him. He was Southern, after all, and any born-and-bred Georgia boy worth his salt would recognize the distinct metallic click of a 12-gauge shotgun. And given the decided assuredness of the action, he knew whoever had him in their sights was familiar with the gun and, more important, knew how to use it.

"On your feet, hands where I can see them," she ordered. He had to hand it to her. Sophie O'Brien was cool as a cucumber. Her voice was steady, not betraying the slightest bit of fear. Which, irrationally, irritated him. He was a strange man trespassing on her property—she ought to be afraid, dammit. Why hadn't she stayed in the house and called 911 like a normal woman?

Oh, right, he thought sarcastically. Because she wasn't a *normal* woman. She was kind and confident, fiendishly clever and sexy as hell.

He wanted her.

And the hell of it? Aside from the conflict of interest and the tiny matter of *her name at the top of his suspect list?*

She didn't like him.

"Move," she said again, her voice firmer. "I'd rather not shoot you, but I will if you don't stand up and turn around."

Beautiful, Jeb thought, feeling extraordinarily stupid. He'd been an army ranger, one of the fiercest soldiers among Uncle Sam's finest…and he'd been bested by a massage therapist with an Annie Oakley complex.

With a sigh, he got up and flashed a grin at her. "Evening, Sophie. Your shrubs need mulching."

She gasped, betraying the first bit of surprise. It was ridiculous how much that pleased him. "You?" she breathed. "What the hell are you doing out here?"

He pasted a reassuring look on his face and gestured to the gun still aimed at his chest. "Would you mind lowering your weapon? It's a bit unnerving."

She brought the barrel down until it was aimed directly at his groin. "There," she said, a smirk in her voice. "Feel better?"

Has Jebb finally met his match? Find out in
THE PROFESSIONAL

Available November 2012
wherever Harlequin Blaze books are sold.

Find yourself
BANISHED TO THE HAREM
in a glamorous and tantalizing new tale from

Carol Marinelli

Playboy Sheikh Prince Rakhal Alzirz has time for
one more fling in London before he must return
to his desert kingdom—and Natasha Winters has
caught his eye. He seizes the chance to discover if
Natasha is as fiery in bed as her flaming red hair,
but their recklessness has consequences.... She
might be carrying the Alzirz heir!

BANISHED
TO THE HAREM

Available October 16!